I0677593

The Well from Hell

by

Wes Anderson

Western Country Enterprise's LLC, May 14 2017
Copyright © by Wes Anderson

ISBN-13:978-0998758602
ISBN-10: 0998758604
LLCN: 2017902944

BISAC: Fiction / Mystery & Detective / General

About the author:

Wes Anderson grew up in Texas and as a young man left The Lone Star State to find his way in Wyoming, Montana and North Dakota. Wes has held many positions in the oilfield over the last decade, starting on drillings rigs and making his way to running completion and fishing tools. He started writing "The Well from Hell" in 2015 when the slowdown hit. "There were just so many memories and experiences from the Bakken and nobody is telling them, its time they are heard."

Wes owns Branding Iron BBQ with his wife in Dillon, MT and is currently working on his second oilfield novel.

This book is dedicated to Timmy, a brother of the field that I was privileged to have worked alongside a many of nights and tripped a many miles of pipe with. To you and all other fallen brothers. You are missed.

A story of the Bakken

Synopsis

Wyatt, a charismatic oilfield downhole specialist who had been laid off during the downturn of 2009, gets called back in to take on a new set of downhole problems in Williston, North Dakota. Wyatt teams up with the knowledgeable but ornery well specialist Zebb Morgan, a man who has forgotten more than Wyatt will ever know about the oilfield. Follow their struggle to repair an oil well that seems to be connected straight to the pit of hell as they fight blowouts, putting their lives on the line while they race to free millions of dollars of oil tools stuck thousands of feet beneath the earth's surface.

The Well from Hell is an insightful and enticing tale that will keep you turning the page. It depicts the adventures of oilmen and the struggles they go through to get oil out of the hell that holds it. It's a story of the Bakken Boom. Walk with Wyatt and Zebb as things go from bad to worse while trying to solve the mystery of downhole drilling.

CHAPTER 1
Late October of 2010

Pick-up lines are for suckers. A woman worth taking out has heard the same lines a hundred times. I neared the Horse section of literature in the library of University Montana Western in my small town of Dillon—and I had never even been on a horse, definitely never felt ambitious enough to read about one of the crazy animals, they scared me to death— crossing into uncharted waters one aisle at a time as I watched her searching book after book. Her hourglass hips filling out jeans in pure cowgirl fashion caught my eye, but it was her sunrise-dirty blond hair that drove me to approach. I felt myself unable to retreat even though she was engulfed in her reading, frantically flipping pages looking for something— something that was definitely not me. I tried to think of what to say as my eye suddenly caught sight of competition. A young man dressed in ironed, light-brown khakis with a pompadour haircut combed deep to his left side approached her. I kept mine short and covered my morning laziness with a faded ball cap from my days in the oilfield. He introduced himself to her and I overheard my new nemesis' name, Skylar. I felt my heart sink as I realized that I might have just missed my chance. He probably was quite the scholar, for all I knew, and in a competition for a college-educated woman in a library full of subjects I had never studied. I suddenly felt inadequate standing in my tattered oil stained blue jeans and ball cap, wondering what my chances were even before this random guy showed up.

By the look of his carefully combed hair, this seemed

to be his day; he looked to be on Cloud Nine, and my stomach started to turn. I was beginning to feel out of place. I drew closer to them and realized I had no real plan here; all I knew was his name from the introduction I had overheard. I had no clue who this guy even was, but whatever the case, she didn't seem overly interested in what he was saying.

My steps drew closer and it promptly dawned on me that I still had a chance, my chance to not have to talk about horses or come up with some stupid pick-up line. I hurried down the aisle and abruptly interrupted them. With my hand on his shoulder and blocking his view and conversation with the clearly irritated beauty, I stuck my paw out for him to shake. "I'm Wyatt, good to meet you, Skylar," I said and waited for his response. As he finally shook my hand, I could sense his confusion; his shake felt like a dead fish, which brought me some comfort. I knew I didn't have to worry about him stealing her away from me anytime soon.

"Um, good to meet you. Me and this lovely lady were working on an interview for her thoughts on the school..." His demeanor was confused. Why was I bothering him? I guess he just didn't see the whole picture.

"Well, that's what I needed to talk with you about, Skylar. I've been looking all over campus for you. I was sent here from Professor Lanton to interview with you for the school reviews and any other question the brightest of minds have come up with. I've really got to get going soon. If we could get this thing over with, that would be great."

"I'm kind of in the middle of something right now. I believe we should get together another time." I couldn't blame him for wanting to talk with her over me, but the fact was that I truly didn't care.

"Look! If you want to go up with me and talk to Professor Lanton, we can do that, but I have thirty minutes before I fly out to do a study in Alaska." I was almost as surprised as he was that I was going to Alaska in 30 minutes, and I wondered if there was actually a Professor Lanton. Whatever the case, it was all or nothing; this was my Hail Mary.

Like a disappointed child, he looked at her as she shrugged her shoulders and politely spoke up. "Sorry." She turned away and continued her pursuit to save the equine world. Skylar looked over at me, frustrated that I was still standing there. I steered him over to a side table and we sat across from one another, with me grabbing the gunfighter's seat in order to have a clear view of her and the library door.

So, this guy had questions, and I had answers. Apparently, the school had recruited him to ask a thousand questions. They wanted to know all sorts of things—how college life was in the dorms, how the food was on campus, what the college could do to attract more students, and what students thought about the degrees offered.

I laid it on thick, even for me. I told him anything I could think of to buy her some time and keep him distracted. I recruited for lower tuition, southern food in the cafeteria, lower taxes, a new president, a new vice-president, a new secretary of state, and fewer gun laws. I laid out my views on racism and our division as a nation, and then hit him with freedom of religion, higher oil prices with lower gasoline prices, and my view on the future of natural gas prices. I told him all the great things I expected out of this college—its faculty and its students—and what enormous potential there was here. I recruited for granite with copper borders on the sidewalks, and, if they could spare it, a touch of gold for the cracks. In the midst of my long soliloquy, I watched as she made her way to the front doors of the library. She took a left as the door shut quietly behind her. Meanwhile, Skylar looked back around and noticing his dream had left, stared back at me with a perplexed look on his face, noticing that this conversation had taken a dramatic turn for the worst. Most of this information he could probably not put in the paper. He started to rise out of his chair and bring things to an end, until I gave him the unexpected.

While wagging my finger at him as a father would do to a nine-year-old child, "No, No, No, sir, you will not leave! You sat down to hear my thoughts, and we got a L-O-O-N-N--G way to go, buddy, so sit your caboose on down and listen."

"I thought you had to catch a flight for Alaska?"

"It can wait. You got important school matters here; I don't want you to be cut short."

"Really, it's okay," he said as I grabbed his shoulder firmly. Out of either fear or ignorance, he sat back down while I buffaloed him for another five minutes on oil prices, supply and demand, and Saudi Arabia as a swing producer, not to mention the current currency war with China, but that was enough for him, I guess. He put his pen in his ink-stained shirt pocket and notebook under his arm, and without saying anything, made a beeline for the door. I smirked and followed him, still trying to fulfill my duty. I knew he could hear me because he started to walk faster.

"Don't you want to hear what I think about electric cars and Tesla, or what about hydrogen fuel cells and how this school could make them better, or we could address the cracked bricks on the front of campus? I know a good mason." He wasn't listening, nor was he smiling, and I couldn't totally blame him. I walked far behind him and watched as he swung the glass door open and fled to the right, which I was glad to see. I turned left in pursuit of changing my own world; I found her outside at the pick-up area.

"You waiting on someone?" I deeply hoped she wouldn't say her boyfriend. Even worse, what if she was married? I didn't see a ring, though, so I thought I was safe.

She wore a slight smirk, though whether it was for me or if it was just her natural look, I couldn't tell. "Perhaps." She held her books in the crook of her left arm and put her right hand out in order to shake. "I'm Jessica. How are you?" It took me off guard. I don't know why, exactly. Maybe it was because most of the time, women just let you sit there awkwardly and try to make conversation with them. I shook her hand and felt a strong grip, stronger than what I had offered, close tight on my hand. I quickly tightened my grip. I always shook a woman's hand light, but I had never had one out-shake even a light handshake. Until now.

"I'm Wyatt. Wyatt Kleinfield. Good to meet you." I could feel my smile kick my cheek out of place as she let go of my hand, but the effect of it remained. The shake would have been of little importance to most, but I believed it to be significant; it was not a fierce hand that grabbed mine, it was just firm—very firm, but soft enough to let me know that I was dealing with a woman, not a girl, a very independent woman based on my impression.

"I've been going to school here a little over two years and—" she brandished her smart phone, "—searched every record for professors while I've been waiting here. You do know there is no such professor named Lanton at this school, don't you?" I tried not to gawk at the way she filled out the emerald green in her blouse, but I could not help but notice.

"I can guarantee you that Skylar is finding that out right about now," I said as I forced my eyes up to look at the blue in hers.

"Why did you distract him like that?"

"Seemed like fun," I said.

"No, really."

"To be honest, I was on my way to ask you to dinner when ol' Skylar got to you first, and it was the only thing I could think of."

"I see. Quick on your feet."

"I try."

"Well?"

It took me a second. My head cocked sideways in slight confusion. What was she after? I wanted to slap myself when it finally dawned on me what she was looking for, and I finally stuttered the words out.

"Uh—well, would you like to join me for dinner?" I wondered if I should have tried to sell it a little more, thrown in steak and lobster or promise martinis into the late night. Probably not, though. I figured I had probably already oversold and overstepped my bounds with the whole reporter thing.

She might have been slightly embarrassed, but she didn't show it. "That would be nice." I sensed encouragement from her and wondered if she was riding the same cloud I was riding on.

"Okay." I smiled, my nerves showing through, as I rocked ever so slightly on the balls of my feet. A feeling of relief washed over me, as though I was in the fourth grade again asking the prettiest girl to a dance, and she had just said "Yes."

She returned my smile while she shifted her books. "Okay."

"Seven o'clock, Wednesday, at The Branding Iron sound good?"

Her smile remained and her heart radiated a joy that transferred to me as I heard the most beautiful words a man could hear from a lady who'd just been asked out on a first date. "Sounds good."

"I have to know, though, what you were searching for so intently in the Equine Science section."

"Well, if you must know, my horse back home in Florida has Cushings, and my mother is frantic down there to get a handle on it, so I was searching for any simple knowledge that might help." She turned with a sway and began to saunter off toward her car. As I watched her rhythmic movements recede, I felt my phone start to vibrate and pulled it from my pocket. The name "Bryant Harwin" flashed across the screen. Manager of Anderson Oil Tools? What could he possibly want? Last I knew he was still in Williston, North Dakota, working the Bakken. How he got ahold of me, I had no idea, but I was certain my good friend Toby McGrath had something to do with it. I pushed the button to accept the call.

CHAPTER 2

"How you doing, Wyatt?" The familiar gruff voice of an old friend coming over the phone was good to hear, despite the past.

"Very well. And what do I owe the honor of this call to?" My tone was ice, masking my pleasure at his call, because I knew the call came with conditions.

"Right to the point, I see."

"Indeed."

"We want you to come back to work for us. We have that position open now that you applied for a year ago."

"Oh, really? It sure took you long enough." I had been laid off from Anderson Oil Tools a little under a year ago, and I felt a slight grudge coming to surface.

"Are you still interested in the position or not, you little smartass?" I had to love the bluntness—no beating around the bush, just straight business. I missed it, although I wondered why. Maybe it was just how my mind was wired after many years in the oilfield.

I watched Jessica drive off in the distance before I responded. "Remember that lay off last year? Yeah, I'm kind of in the middle of rebuilding my life right now." Bryant was the one from Anderson who had been forced to pull the trigger; they cut forty percent overnight, and my number got drawn.

"Come on, man, that was nothing personal; it wasn't even my choice of who to lay off."

"We had talked about a transfer just a couple days

before. Whatever happened to that?"

"Wyatt, it just wasn't that easy! Oil was at thirty-eight dollars a barrel, and they were laying off hands worldwide! For Pete's sake, you couldn't even have gone to Africa and worked if you wanted to!" Even though the grudge I bore had surfaced, it wasn't necessarily for Bryant, it was for the industry as a whole. But I knew that is just how it goes during a downturn.

"Why the hell would I want to?" I had to rib him just a little; Africa would kind of suck, I imagined.

"That's not the point."

"Yeah, but kind of funny to think about, and plus, I think I could get a job in Africa if necessary."

"Maybe feeding monkeys or letting kids sink you in a dumping pool after teaching them to throw a baseball."

"Screw off. Actually, I got a tugboat offer the other day to work out of South Africa."

"Oh, really? Have you ever driven a tugboat?"

"Nope."

"Have you ever been on a tugboat?"

"Nope, but how hard can it be?"

"Do you know anybody who has a tugboat? 'Cause I'm quite curious how this came up. Were you just cruising around town and somebody ran into you and thought you would make a spectacular tugboat operator, or were you searching for mail order brides online and found a tugboat job posting? I mean, really, how in the hell did you get a tugboat offer in Africa?"

"I got a buddy in Montana who has a tugboat business."

"So, let me get this straight. You got a friend who

owns tugboats in Africa but lives in Montana, which I will happily remind you is not on any shore line, and he just so happens to want you to run his tugboat on the coast of South Africa?" He paused for a second to process the opportunity competing with the one he was offering, then he gave me his best rejoinder. "Well, then, go ride the fucking tugboat."

I could hear him chuckling for old times' sake. He sounded like he missed an old friend, but it also sounded like he was probably wondering why in the hell he even made this call once he realized that I might be actually thinking about the tugboat offer. My heart had semi moved on.

"I would but I'm too busy getting dunked in a fucking pool, bobbing for apples to master the whole tugboat art at this time, but when that slows up you will be the first to know."

"You coming to work or not, Wyatt?" There was no frustration in his voice, just matter-of-fact expectation. I could tell his patience was starting to run thin, but he knew what he was in for when he dialed me; it was business as usual, just two old friends catching up, but there was also money on the line.

"What you got?" I asked.

"We're growing busier by the day in Williston, and I need some experience up here; you would be working with Zebb Morgan."

"Cut the sales pitch, what's the money like? And why Zebb Morgan? We usually both work alone."

"The money is fair and getting better. Oil is nearing $80 a barrel and looks to keep rising. As you know, Zebb is getting up there in his ripe old age. He will be retiring shortly, and our plan is to have tool hands that can run fishing tools but also run packers and completion tools, and seeing as how you already got the packer and completion experience, we thought it might be good for y'all to work together on some jobs before he decides to take up a different kind of fishing and play 18 holes all day. I thought it would do well by you, and plus, there's not many who can get along with Zebb."

"And you think I can?"

"Wyatt, I'm well aware of the last job y'all did together, and it seemed to work out just fine. In fact, I seem to remember y'all had a hell of a time."

"That's his side of the story. I almost ended up in jail 'cause of that goofy old man."

"Yeah, but it worked out, didn't it?"

I knew what he was trying to do; he was trying to coax me into agreeing with him, to let my defenses down. They get you to start agreeing to something light and readily true just to get you used to giving in. I was having no part of it, and I had no desire to answer questions about that night. For all I knew, we were still wanted for it.

"His opinion." I suppose it was the most neutral answer I could think of, not a very good one, I knew, but neutral, nonetheless. At least I didn't give him any confirmation.

"Take some time and chew on it. It's a big decision, but I promise you it would be quite the experience. We got some good wells going over here."

"Don't you know North Dakota sucks?"

"My wife tells me that every day, my friend. Every single day."

I knew that to be true from one of my visits with them when his wife Cady made the mistake of having one too many glasses of wine. I had to hand it to her, though; they were quite settled in New Mexico, friends and all, and I mean real friends, not low-life oil junkies like me, and they gave it all up to live the dream in the Bakken. I still couldn't figure out if it was worth it or not for them, but I was happy to have him there. His experience came in handy in the Bakken.

"I will think it over. Give me a couple days to chew on it, and I'll get back to you."

"Sounds good, Wyatt. Talk with you later."

"All right, Bryant, talk with you in a couple days."

"Oh, yeah, I almost forgot, Wyatt, what's her name?"

"Whose name?"

"Your newfound love who's making you question such an opportunity."

"There's no one."

He knew I was lying as soon as it left my lips. I could feel the doubt coming out of the receiver as he spoke. "Yeah, sure. A year ago if I would have offered this to you, you would have been over here tonight."

"All right, All right. Her name is Jessica. And nobody ever said anything about being in love."

"You just did, and plus, no one has to, you can read it in your hesitation, not wanting to come back to North Dakota and make some real money instead of staying in Montana frying brisket."

"We don't fry it."

"Don't lie to me! You boys from the south fry everything. I could give you fried armadillo tail, and you would beer batter it up and fry it again."

"Well, I guess that's part-way true."

"Tell you what, if you need any relationship advice, or just somebody to knock your head on straight, call me. I've been through my fair share."

"Thanks, but I think I'll be all right. I'll figure it out." I didn't know how I felt about the relationship advice. Had it been anyone else, I would probably tell him to just get bent and mind his own business. I knew he meant well, but the fact remained that it hit a raw nerve.

"Just be careful, Wyatt. Don't jump head first on this one, and damn sure don't disappear off to Africa. It was hard enough to get ahold of you in Montana."

"It was Toby that gave you my number, wasn't it?"

He chuckled, sincerely wished me luck, and hung up. Damn Toby! Regardless, I knew he was looking out for me. We had always looked after one another—that's what brothers of the field do. I had changed my number and knew that the only person who had it was Toby since we had grown up together in South Texas and worked Wyoming and North Dakota together. I specifically remember giving him strict instructions to not give it to anyone, and I meant anyone! Even though I liked the hell out of Bryant—and would have loved to have talked to him about anything other than the oilfield—I just didn't want to be bothered with it anymore. Things were changing, and I didn't seem to fit in anymore. A brotherhood was starting to disappear and was being replaced with rules and regulation. However, the simple fact remained that after one five-minute phone call from Bryant, I was seriously contemplating getting back in.

CHAPTER 3
The Next Day: 3 P.M.

I trekked higher into the Blacktail mountains outside of Dillon, Montana, feeling the crunch of snow beneath my boots. I stopped and reached into my back pocket and pulled out my flask, feeling the warmth of cinnamon Schnapps as I took a slug. I took in the view in all of its glory; the mountains roamed into one another without end. They had already started stacking their winter coat and held a sensational view. These mountains sank deep in my soul—there was healing out here that you couldn't find in a thousand cities. I took one more slug and let the Schnapps warm my empty stomach. I had to make it to the top to find whatever awaited me; I hoped it held the answer of which direction to take in my fork in the road. I felt pure peace. There were no crystal balls at the top of the ridge, but there was the stillness of the wilderness— decision-making territory. The sun was starting to meet the clouds, and sweat was starting to meet the back of my neck as I continued my climb higher. I felt my thighs straining in agony with every step, but it felt good, and it was only here that I could think clearly, no matter the strain. I felt rocks loosen under my soles as they began a quick roll to the bottom. I took a deep breath and watched as rocks bigger than my fist found their way down, snowballing smaller rocks with them as they went. The mountains near Dillon were beautiful; they had a special aura about them I couldn't describe. Some said they weren't as nice as the majestic Tetons, others said they were better, but to me they were always better because that's the place I called home, and I could freely roam.

I sat down my pack under a pine and reached for my battered, leather-bound journal. Even an oil man has to write to clear his soul. I lay back against a boulder and propped my legs as old cowboys do in the pictures, right leg up and crossed over the left to make the perfect square. I untied the twine that held my journal together as I pulled a pen from a side pocket and started to write.

"Life Journal"

Lord,

You have given me more than enough; you have sent me from Texas to Wyoming, then up to North Dakota working in your fields. But I'm confused. Why the layoff? Why the temptation to get back in? I had no intention of going back once I packed my bags in North Dakota, work or not; it just wasn't where I wanted to be, even though I loved the field. The field had given so much to me as a young man—not just financial pleasures; it had practically raised me. They took me into their pack as one of their own, and all I had to do was prove my effort. You used the field to teach me, to mold me. I have long read of boys turning to men back in the day on long cattle drives to the west, learning to ride and rope from the older cowboys. My situation was not much different from theirs, and it seemed to me I was chasing the same, flying out west on my own, except this time I was climbing oil rigs, not roping cows, but the search for a young man's soul was still the same. When the oilfield work dried up, and with my recent divorce, I felt your calling to get on with life. With no home to go home to, somehow you positioned me in Dillon, Montana.

Lord, are you asking me to leave Dillon for the oilfield? I like Dillon, small but just right for me. With not a rig in sight, my mind was at ease. I can rest here—the mountains and pines give me that. Almost a year has gone by since I have been laid off. I enjoy my job at The Branding Iron smoking prized brisket. Our BBQ is world class, and the smoke pulls people in like a tugboat from the deep south. There is life to be lived here, but something in me is itching to get back in the oil game. I'm drawn to it, like a moth to flame. Some things can't be explained. Is this you calling me back to the field?

I have heard that times are tough right now in the patch. The price of oil seems to be recovering though, getting close to $80 a barrel. I find myself torn, yin and yang. One day I want to be the next T-Boone Pickens, and the next, I just want to be in a cabin in the pines of Montana. The call from Bryant has me torn. Lord is this your way?

The conversation with Bryant played in my mind as I closed the worn leather cover and let the last of my thoughts linger on the end of a page. I thought on the opportunity as snow flurries began to settle against the caramel-colored hide of my journal. It was no doubt a fork in the road as well as a gamble. Zebb was one of the best, well-traveled and well-versed. I wondered if I could keep up with the knowledge he had from his years spent working wells. I wondered if it would be worth it. I knew I would be giving up what I had come to love—freedom, mountain air, and the smooth scent of pines that soothed the distress in my soul. I wondered if I could make it work with Jessica if she and I hit it off. Could I find the sacred balance of love and oil? The field could transform a person. If I took the job, I would go after it with everything I had on a dead run and nothing would hold me back. I sorted out the options as if they rested on a balance measuring precious decisions. The question remained as to why I wanted to work in a field that almost killed me once before, a field that took from me everything I had, but in a strange way also supplied everything too.

My watch neared five, and I tapped it in hopes that it would change. My mind was starting to go numb over the lack of entertainment and my own thoughts. I trekked down feeling at peace, but weighing in the balance, a beauty awaited who threatened to upset all of my plans.

CHAPTER 4
7 p.m.

I watched her pull her baby blue sedan between the two yellow lines at seven p.m. on the dot. She had refused to let me pick her up. I guess she wanted to be prepared in case the date went bad—no one could blame her for that. Her black dress fit tight against the curves of her hips and fell just above the knees—modest, but high enough to spark an interest. Her short, dirty hair blew from a slight breeze of cold wind as she calmly walked toward me. We warmly greeted each other and walked the corners of downtown until we arrived at The Branding Iron. I pulled the solid oak door open and let her in. The room sat a dark maroon on the walls and hung pictures of magnificent elk and laced with rawhide rope for trim and custom wooden bar tops and tables that sat all around us. It was BBQ at its finest, their brisket was first class and their ribs pulled gently off the bone with a sauce that would knock your socks off. The owners were from the deep south and had brought their taste buds up to Montana in which I was thankful for. The hostess Courtney which was one of the owners sat us at a candle-lit corner table set for two and told us our waitress would be with us shortly. We usually never had a hostess nor a waitress nor a table set, it wasn't the way BBQ was traditionally done but they had seemed to pull out all the stops after I called. I looked around at the empty room realizing that it was just Jessica and myself as we made small talk and I looked at the window and read a sign backwards as it was designed for guest to read from the front while trying to come in, *Sorry we are closed for a private party.*

Soon she appeared from the back, dressed in a classic crisp, white button-up with her dark brown hair tied in a ponytail. She introduced herself as Sarah, in which I of course knew as we had worked together for the last several months and I felt a slight tinge in my stomach as I remembered lightly flirting with her during work hours. She politely asked about our evening, then for our drink order. I gestured for Jessica to go first.

"You got sweet tea?" she asked.

"We do." Sarah replied. Jessica looked surprised.

"I will take that then."

Sarah nodded toward her as she wrote down and then smiled. "Will do."

I hadn't heard many people ask for sweet tea up here, but it was a request that I could appreciate. It made me remember home, remember Grandma's fridge down south that seemed to always hold a pitcher of sweet tea—the same fridge that held Blue Bell Ice cream and Dr. Pepper. That was without a doubt the best fridge on earth, I was certain. Jessica unknowingly had triggered my thoughts of home and so had The Branding Iron, maybe that's why I ended up working there. It seemed silly, but I knew that some part of me wanted to experience home once again.

I wondered if the tea would truly satisfy her southern taste buds. I noticed a hopeful smile break out as she pulled the menu closer to her to get a better look at the entrées. Sarah turned to me for my order.

"Rum and coke." Sarah smiled towards me and nodded.

Sarah left, giving us time to glance at the menu even though I already knew what I wanted but the interest for both of us was not on the menu nor the food. My focus was on a woman whose focus was on me. This was nice, something I hadn't felt in quite a while.

"S-o-o-o, Wyatt, what brings you to town anyhow? You are obviously not a college student."

"Why do you say that?" It was a logical question. I felt slightly insulted, although I would have died before signing up to attend college. Still, I wanted to know why she thought I couldn't be a student.

She sat back and lowered her head, glancing in her lap and letting her hands drop to her thighs. She adjusted her napkin and looked back at me as her hair splayed over her shoulder. "I just don't see it."

"You mean I don't strike you as the next intellectual biology wizard or a guy on a waiting list for IBM, or maybe the next mechanical genius to save the Hoover Dam?" I was mildly offended and leaned forward and adjusted my silverware, wondering how this would play out. Why would she not consider me a student? Did I come off as that uneducated? I wondered if, after all, this would turn out to be a very short dinner.

"Not necessarily. You're different than the boys in school. You hold yourself in a different manner that I can't really put my finger on—not bad, just different—plus, you couldn't come up with a real name for a professor, and I couldn't find you in any of our student records." I rubbed my goatee and sank in thought. She presented a very valid point. She probably couldn't find me because I never signed up or signed in or whatever you do if you join the penitentiary they call college.

She had said it with class, at least. I have always had a

deep-rooted sore spot about college deep inside me. I burned through those high school doors right after graduation, disgusted with the system and determined to never return to it; plus, it didn't help that college was shoved down my throat from birth. If it had been anyone else, I would have told her to go get plucked, but she was asking while wearing a sleek black dress that hugged all the parts of her that I was aching to hug myself. Also, her figuring out the whole professor thing explained her take on things; she had a very valid argument.

"I guess you found me out. I'm not quite a student, at least not of the college, and I'm more of less just in town for a little while." Not the most pleasing of answers, but it's what I had, and it's what I knew to be true.

"Doing what?"

"Just kind of hanging out right now, taking it easy."

"I see," she said, sounding unimpressed. I figured the image of a ski bum or beach bum flashed through her mind, a guy bouncing around from state to state, coast to coast, trying the mountains one year, back to the beach for the next. She was probably wondering if I was going to be able to pay for this meal or if she would be washing dishes when the meal was over.

Sarah stepped in and politely tried to take our order again, but we weren't ready. She sat the glasses down on the knotty pine table and promised to return in a few minutes. I hoped the rum would ease my nerves, but I wasn't sure if it could quite do its job tonight. I watched as Jessica took the first sip of sweet tea as if in a tasting contest and nodded her head in approval.

I took the first sip of rum and coke and felt the burn in the back of my throat. All was right in the world, at least for this very moment. I sat the glass back on the pine, but kept my hand on it. A beautiful woman in front of me and a chilled glass of rum in my hand. I had been a bundle of nerves all day, nervous about taking her out. She was out of my league, out of my class, yet here she was right in front of me. Maybe I was nervous because I knew I would probably screw it up at some pivotal point. No matter. I smiled and reached for my glass and took another swig of rum and felt my nerves start to loosen.

"What you thinking about getting?" I asked.

"Not quite sure yet. I was looking at the salads."

"You got to get more than a salad, or I'm not going to feel like I've done my job tonight." My pocketbook probably didn't share the sentiment, but to not to treat her like royalty tonight would've put me in misery and obviously ruined any outside chance I had with this queen, no question about it.

She laughed. "Well, maybe the salad was just for starters before I ordered the lobster with a side of ribeye." I took a double take as I knew The Branding Iron didn't regularly serve ribeye's and lobster but sure enough it was hand written in on *The Special* section at the bottom of the menu along with *Smoked Salmon*.

I gestured for her to proceed and polished off my glass of rum. That last sip went down strong. "Go ahead, that does sound good. If you order it, make it two." She smiled and I returned it with one of my own. I secretly hoped she was joking about the lobster and ribeye—it ran upwards of $50 a plate, but if not, so be it. At least I knew if it came from The Branding Iron it would be good. Sarah made it back to our table. While we sat acting like giddy middle schoolers, and I wondered what she made of it.

"Is your smoked salmon wild or raised?" Jessica asked.

"Wild. We get it shipped in every Friday from Alaska. Never been frozen."

"That's good to know. Sockeye or Coho?"

"Coho." Sarah replied.

"I'll take the salmon then, with a side of salad." She knew what she wanted, and I liked it. Being decisive was not a bad thing by any means in my book, and salmon definitely was a good choice.

"I will take the brisket with a sweet potato, and another rum and coke would be great." I chimed in.

"Half and half?"

"Yes, please." There was no mistaking that Jessica noticed that I had just ordered a second drink before the meal had even hit the table. She didn't seem to mind; she wore the look of a mother when her favorite son is going after a second cookie for dessert, simply taking note with a watchful eye. I guess it wasn't just her that had my nerves in a knot. The decision of going back to Williston still weighed heavily on me. We made small talk as Sarah set my refill on the pine, and I subconsciously sipped till it sat half full.

"Half empty or half full?" Jessica teased. I slid my glass to the center of the table and watched as her slender hand grasped my glass, picked it up, and moved it toward her mouth. She took a sip. And another. And another. She brandished it back and forth and let a smile stretch across her cheeks.

"Empty now." Her deep blue eyes looked right into mine, and I couldn't help but laugh in disbelief. Slightly turned on, I reached out to take my glass from her hand; our fingers met and glided through one another's, and I felt the smoothness of her skin. Then, for a few brief seconds, her fingers gripped mine. The world, for a moment, grew suddenly quiet, at least at our table, as she seemed to realize that she was holding hands with a man she barely knew. She gently released my hand and pulled away, and I took my empty glass back as both of us remained silent. She sat back and resumed her ladylike position.

I was growing more and more curious about the young beauty sitting across from me. "So, since I actually know you are in college, what will your degree be in when you're finished?"

"Biology, business, and animal science."

"That's quite the combination. What does a lady do with a degree like that?"

"Ranch manager, vet school, biologist, stockbroker—possibilities are endless." She smiled a smile that warmed my soul; she knew she was dreaming big, and I did too, and I liked it. It was a rarity.

"I guess let me rephrase. What are you going to be doing with this endless degree?"

"To be honest, after I get done here, I'm headed to Colorado or back home to Florida for Vet school."

"I see. Seems interesting ... and quite expensive."

"We shall see. I got a full ride for going here. We'll see how vet school works out, plus I do photography in the area on the side and commission artwork, so that helps pay the rent."

This woman knew what she wanted. I had heard about these women in tall tales. I'd dreamed of a woman with a real head on her shoulders, a brain inside of a beautiful frame. I wasn't used to a woman with something between the ears, someone who thought about money and life and actually wanted to live it. I just hoped I could keep up. Sarah materialized and set another drink down for me and then vanished just as quickly.

The cold glass had chilled my hand, and the condensation from my glass dripped on the pine, soaking my side of the table. "Ambitious, are we?" I asked as I grasped my napkin and started wiping the water off while waiting for her response.

Her head cocked to the side as she gazed straight at me. "Something wrong with that?"

"No, not at all. Just admiring it. It's a rarity." I decided to try and change the conversation to something more lighthearted. I searched my mind for a topic. "So, how is Florida?"

"I don't think so. You're not getting off that easy. I just told you my passions, dreams, and potentially where I will be living, and you gave me nothing, absolutely nothing but a question about my home state. Let's back up and let me ask a few questions of my own." You could feel the playfulness mixed with a seriousness beam from her—she meant business. She wanted to know who I was, and she was not going to be put off; plus, she was far too pretty not to answer, and I'm sure she knew it. I again admired her blond hair falling on her shoulders and her dress that she filled out ever so tightly as it hugged against her breast. A black bra strap peeked out of her dress and sat beside the freckles on her shoulder, and I wondered if she knew the strap was out of place. I assumed she didn't because she seemed the type to tuck it back in, but no matter, the fact that it remained visible was sexy and exciting. I thought of her as a woman waiting to be discovered, and I felt privileged to be across from her. Her thigh-high slit dress would have been enough to pry anything out of any man; I would have voluntarily surrendered my social security card, credit card, blank checks—she just didn't know that I didn't have much to give. I felt like a gambler sitting at a blackjack table looking at a queen and wondering what to do next. I figured if the truth was all that she wanted, then I was getting off easy, so the truth she should have.

"Fair enough. Shoot." I was wide open now, and I knew it. There would be no backing down, no beating around the bush. She was too sharp, too keen, and she was about to dissect my very soul.

"Are you from Montana?"

"Texas."

Surprised, she repeated my response. "Texas?"

"Yep."

Where at in Texas?" She fired her questions off like a lawyer facing me on the stand, and I answered them without reservation. This was it, time to put it all out in the open. From my answers, she would decide right here, right now, if she could move on with this, with me. The truth was that I was scared out of my skin, but I hoped it didn't show. I took a sip, sat my glass down, let the rum soothe my bloodstream, and I pondered where this conversation would lead.

"Houston area," I answered, looking right into her beautiful blue eyes as if I had nothing to hide. "Next?" I took another sip and motioned for her to continue.

"Why did you leave?"

"Two words can explain it all: money and mountains."

"Explain," she prodded, as if she had just gotten a wanted bank robber hiding out in Dillon, Montana, to admit his guilt. She leaned forward, tuning in more carefully.

"Can I give you the short story?"

"As long as you give me something." She wanted something on me. She wanted to know me, but I didn't want to dredge up old wounds. I wanted to bury my past; I wanted to bury my soul. I wished she would let me, just let me get through the night, let me enjoy one night without being anguished, let me just enjoy her company. Why wouldn't she let me? Why was she pushing so hard on a first date? Was my past really that important to her? Apparently, it was.

I smiled in disbelief at the thought of her wanting to get to know me. Somewhere down deep, I had convinced myself that no one really wanted to get to know me.

"Okay, let's start from the beginning, well...at least senior year, when I consider my life to have actually begun. You see, I was looking to start my career working at a diesel mechanic shop as a shop hand. But I looked around, and all I saw were some of the hardest-working men I had ever known, highly skilled in their trade, who had done it all their lives and were still struggling to make ends meet and actually have a halfway decent life. They drove nice cars, their houses were mostly brick, and they had the good life in suburban neighborhoods, but looks can be deceiving, most were living on credit or borrowed time. If they would lose a job they would probably lose their house the next week! It didn't make sense to me, none of it did, the city, the skyscrapers in Houston. It was just how I saw life around me at that time through my young eyes. We were lucky that Mont Belvieu didn't need the whole skyscraper thing, but the people, and most of all, the neighborhoods, just seemed trapped. I felt like a child stuck inside a box with no way out—"

"—still in the Houston area?" she interrupted, in order to orient herself. I frowned at the interruption until I realized that she had done so because she was genuinely interested. It was a change of pace from the immature girls I was used to, girls who grew up having life given to them and the world revolving around them and who seemed to have been taught to take advantage of any man who actually cared about them.

"Thirty miles east of Houston, in a town of about four thousand people: Mont Belvieu. It used to be a farming community until Katarina happened, and it seemed to just go downhill from there."

"Refugees?"

"Yeah, if you want to call them that. There were some really good people who came over, but there were also some real trash who came there since we were on the outskirts of Houston."

I paused and let the rum course through my bloodstream and steady my nerves so that my body could relax. I pondered the philosophical and economic theory of a blue-collar man trying to provide for his family. I sipped my drink while trying to decide the best way to convey my life to her, and I wondered when I finally spit it out if judgment might come. "My parents divorced, and I got engaged at the age of 17 to my high school sweetheart." I saw her face cloud up as if I had just dropped a bomb on her, which I guess in many ways I did. It was a lot to come out with in just one sentence, but I figured to get it all out there on the table. I wondered if she would walk out.

"You were engaged?" She seemed shocked, as if I had purposely hidden it from her, as if I had reached across the table and slapped her in the face.

"I knew you were going to latch on to that." I said quietly, slightly ashamed.

"Well, where is she?" She probably wondered if she was having dinner with a married man.

"Divorced and gone." As I dredged up the past, I felt my heart sink when reminded of that lost love. I sipped my rum and set my glass back down on the table while she leaned back in thought and bit her lip. The way this was going, I would be out of rum in no time. I honestly didn't care about what happened the rest of the night. Right now it was all on the line; she would either deal with it or she wouldn't. Whatever her choice, I had bigger choices on my mind. The oilfield was still calling to me, and the success of this date was starting to seem like the least of my worries, especially if she kept making me resurrect old bones all night because of her questions.

"What brought you up north, then?" Apparently, she wasn't done asking questions, but I was glad she dropped the divorce. I wondered if she had seen the hurt in my eyes. I could barely look at her. I was glad to not have to dwell on it. Besides, what business was it of hers? I didn't even have to tell her—if anything, volunteering the information should have shown her that I wasn't hiding anything. I shook my head to clear the mental fog and repeated her question, buying myself time.

"What brought me up north?"

"Yes, what brought you to Montana?" It was a logical enough question.

I shrugged and smirked, then took another sip and felt myself becoming slightly numb. The rum was doing its work. "Like I said, money and mountains."

She smiled at the simple logic. "There has to be more to it than that." There was, but something inside me held back. It was a lot to give out on a first date, and the fact was that I wanted lighthearted conversation, but it seemed she wasn't going to let that happen. I bit the inside of my lip and chewed a slight piece of flesh off as I swirled my glass and looked down, thinking about what to tell her and what not tell her. I took another sip and felt the alcohol burn my lip on the skin where the missing flesh had been, and I realized there was no more time to buy and no way to get out of talking about myself.

"I was working for my family moving furniture, and we just so happened to be moving a guy out of a large house into a larger house who told me about there being a natural gas boom up north in Wyoming, so I went."

"Just like that, you went? Just got off of work and hopped in your truck and was there the next day. Just like that?"

"Pretty much. I packed up with my wife at the time and headed out. I mean, I said my prayers and loaded up the few things I owned in the motor home I'd only had for a couple of months, cashed out my savings, a whopping total of two thousand dollars, and headed north. The only three things I knew were what the guy said, the newspapers saying rig hands were making between twenty-six and forty-eight dollars an hour, and Wyoming was north of me. I figured I could do it and headed out, not having a clue what a rig hand actually did, but I knew I could do it. Before I left, I had an old boss tell me I was headed for Worm's Corner —which I had no idea what that meant. Later I found out just exactly what it meant when I signed on to a rig company and was instructed that I was the new worm on the crew, the lowest of the low that knew absolutely nothing and got every possible shit job available. It was later that I found out there was a bigger part to being a roughneck than what I actually knew. As some have said, I was a roughneck before I knew what roughnecking was; it was a mindset thing, not a career thing. The mindset of knowing that you can do the job no matter the size or the task, the mindset of using anything or anybody to get it done no matter what the cost, the mindset of leaving everything you have ever known or loved just to better yourself—that's part of the mindset that makes up a good roughneck. Of course, other times it means being a hundred foot up a rig, latching up stands of drill collars while hanging on for dear life to the edge while it's thirty below zero."

She looked right into my hazel eyes, trying to figure me out while struggling with her thoughts. "So you basically headed up north, got divorced, then got involved with the oilfield, all at the age of eighteen."

"No, I got involved with the oilfield at the age of eighteen, but didn't get divorced 'til twenty. Just didn't work out." My hand seemed glued to my glass as I raised it to my lips. I wished she would shut up about my divorce.

"So why did you decide to go strictly to the oilfield and not keep at house building or mechanic or something like that?" I was happy to move away from the divorce subject—the farther the better in my book. She didn't need to know everything in one night, did she? It wasn't her life. Just let me have one pleasant dinner without having to explain why I was left on some cold, bitter, lonesome winter night. I'd rather her leave and let me finish the rum and dinner alone than have to keep rehashing memories that I was still trying to bury.

"Well, to be honest, I never really thought about it much, I guess. Drilling rigs just always drew me to them. They seemed challenging, something different. It seems like everyone named Joe and Mike can build a house or work on a car, but not everyone can fix a situation ten thousand feet downhole or fish out five thousand feet of corroded tubing eaten up by hydrogen sulfide."

"Really? You never truly thought about why you moved across the country and risked everything? I don't buy it. You had to have reached a point in your life where you said, 'This is what I'm going to do, come hell or high water, this is it and so be it,' there just had to be."

She was a gem, far more valuable than gold, and she didn't even know it. I think that was the sexiest thing about it—a woman by herself driven by her own mission, a woman driven for more than herself. My only thought was how to make her driven for me.

"I do have one slight story if you want to hear it."

She gestured for me to go ahead. It felt so good to want to be heard. I've never been one to enjoy the sound of my own voice by any means, but to have someone that generally seemed to care about my thoughts—well, I had not experienced that before. It was surreal and shocking and comforted my soul.

"I guess If I had to point to one thing that really got me thinking, it would be the day while I was catnapping and failing my chemistry class all at the same time, and I heard the teacher ask the class, "If you could have your choice between a well that needed to be pumped or a well that flowed on its own, which one would you choose?" The whole class raised their hand for the one that needed to be pumped. I couldn't believe it! I was almost appalled at the stupidity of the smartest people in the room. I quickly raised my hand for the one that was free-flowing. It was the only thing that made sense to me, plus, what did I have to lose, I was already failing. I couldn't shake the idea of having a well free-flowing without a pump. That seemed like the greatest cash flow ever, and these guys wanted to stick a pump on it. I was the only one that raised my hand, and everybody looked at me stupidly until the teacher said I was right. Then I went back to sleep until senior year."

"And the rest is pretty much history, I take it?"

"Pretty much."

I swirled my glass and took my last sip, watching the half-melted cubes fall back to the bottom. I knew it would be unwise to order a fourth, especially on a first date. My thoughts drifted to possibly going back to North Dakota even though my decision had been made in the first three seconds of the phone call from Bryant. I just had to convince my heart to go along with it, and I wondered how I would tell Jessica and if I would be able to get a second date with her if I burned off to North Dakota.

She was done with her sweet tea, and she glanced with a slightly sad smile at her empty glass and looked over at mine. I wore a similar expression as we eyed the empty glasses, and I wondered if they resembled our hearts.

"So how long before you think we get refills?" she asked. I felt the slight touch of her dress flats press against my shin as she asked. They weren't quite as exotic as high heels but matched perfectly with her black dress, and as their name suggested, they were quite flat on the bottom. The sole moving over and rubbing against the side of my calf shocked me and excited every living nerve in my body. Her foot slid to my inner thigh, but the contact quickly disappeared. She never broke a smile to reveal her intentions. Did she mistake my leg for the table? Was she slightly embarrassed now? I couldn't get a read on her, and it frustrated me. I wondered if I had just missed an opportunity for at the very least a returning flirt. The touch seemed so genuine—maybe it was the way her foot glided halfway up my calf and then back down, maybe it was the nonchalance of the whole thing. Or had I mistaken it? Whatever the case, I believed the best play was the safest because the last thing I needed to do was mistake the gesture as a lovemaking call and return it with vigor.

"Not long; they are usually pretty good about it here."

She leaned forward and placed her elbow on the table and rested her chin on her palm as she looked straight at me and gave a hint of a smile. "I see. Do you take all the college girls out here?"

"Just the ones that I plan to bring back a second time." She was trying to get a read on me. I could sense it. I imagine she was wondering if she was just another girl or if this date meant something to me. The truth was that this date did mean something to me, I just wasn't quite sure why or how much.

She smirked at my comment and possibly my ego. "Ha, you think there will be a second? What makes you so confident?" I wanted to tell her it was because she had provocatively just rubbed my calf and up to my thigh, but I knew that would kill the sentiment and totally dull the mood.

"Why wouldn't there be? You seem to have good taste

too." I knew I was walking a fine line between confident and cocky; the comment was borderline, but I believed the statement to be true. Her eyes reflected disbelief at my audacity. With an exasperated look, she laughed, probably thinking I was only being me, which was true.

"I told you quite a bit about myself, but all I really know about you is that you used to live in Florida, you aspire to be a vet, you have a horse in Florida that is sick, and you keep in contact with your mother. That's really not much to go off of."

"You want something more than that? I thought that to be quite a lot."

"Yes, I do want more. I guess that's a fault of mine." I grinned impishly at the double meaning. I did want more. It was a trait of mine, it just wasn't always a good trait. However, it definitely has its advantages sometimes.

"Well, I would say that's quite a bit for a first date, but if you must know, I actually have two horses in Florida, and the one that is sick—her name is Kona—she has been quite sick for a while, she— Kona is actually my sister's horse, but I claim her. Sonny is mine. I've had him since I was five. He was my first love." She said it with a seriousness that made me wonder if she was crazy and thought herself a horse. Surely not. Everything else about her seemed quite sane, although I knew from family experience that horse people had a little world of their own that only they understood.

"Who was your second?"

"My second what?" I wondered if she answered my question with a question in order to get out of my question or if she did it to buy herself some time in hopes that I was asking something different than what I was.

"Your second love?"

The question hit her hard. She grew quiet and her face grew troubled. Finally, in a small, fragile voice, she muttered, "That's a conversation for another time."

I thought about prying. I was genuinely curious. I wanted to know what made her click and what made her soul come alive. Also, if she had been in love before, maybe she could fall in love again, but she had been nice enough to me to not pry, so I figured I would return the favor. "That sounds good. Sorry I asked."

"It's all right. I just don't feel like talking about it."

"I understand." That was the simple truth, and I wondered as we sat there smiling and drinking if we were both one of the same kind. Had she, like me, given all she had to somebody only to be dumped on? Had she, like me, loved with the deepest part of her heart just to be stabbed in the back by her lover? I wondered if he had cheated or had just not loved her as much as she had loved him. Whatever the case, it went to her core.

I changed the subject. "You got pictures?"

"Pictures of what?"

"Pictures of your horses, silly." she started pulling out her phone to show off her babies almost before I got the words out, like an excited mother showing off her honor roll child. They were gorgeous horses, and I let her know as much as she scrolled through pictures, bragging on Sonny especially, but they did seem to be getting up there in age, and I wondered how long a horse can actually live to be. However, that sure didn't seem like a good question to ask.

The date was going good, and I wanted to keep it that way. In fact, I was almost ready for it to end before I messed it up, something I knew I could do well.

More drinks and the food finally arrived. The Coho was cooked perfectly and my brisket was as tender as anything you could find deep down in Texas. We ate and drank our fill, complementing the food as we went and smiling at each other as if we were teenagers again. Her foot never rubbed my calf again, but things were good.

"Check, please?" I asked as Sarah returned toward the end of our dinner. I turned back to Jessica as Sarah went off to get our bill. "I do have something to tell you."

"What's that?"

The eagerness to talk freely with her scared me, and I wondered if it was the rum kicking in, loosening my lips, but I was committed now that I had spoken up. "I got a decision to make about a job opportunity in North Dakota. I just feel like I should tell you that I may possibly be gone for a while."

"Is it a good offer?"

I nodded ever so slightly and spoke with a more serious tone than what had been used all night by either one of us. "It's an excellent offer, a once-in-a-lifetime offer if things play out how I think they will."

"Do you want it?"

"Well, that's kind of the thing, I'm not really sure yet."

"What are you not sure about?"

"Life in the oilfield and life in Montana are two totally different things, one being better than the other. I will let you take your guess on which one. The oilfield just has a way of dragging you back in."

She glanced down, adjusted her napkin, and brought her eyes back up to stare deep into mine, genuinely curious about what I was talking about. "Tell me about this opportunity."

"I would be working as a completion specialist again; except this time it sounds like I would be running more fishing tools."

I could see the confusion on her face as she waited for me to expound. "What does that entail?"

"The short version is basically I would be getting unwanted and unknown objects out of the hole. For example, when the crew drops a string of pipe ten thousand feet downhole, and it falls to the bottom of a dry well that's extremely gassy, and it flattens like a pancake along with corkscrewing, all while causing a fire downhole that nobody ever sees up at the surface, it's my job to get it all out." She looked semi-impressed, or curious, or maybe she was just surprised that I actually did something else besides pick up college girls in the library.

I went on. "The thing about this opportunity is I would get to work with Zebb Morgan. He's an old-school, backwoods know-it-all, but he is extremely good at his job, and they want us to work together because of our different backgrounds."

"No offense, but if this guy is as good as you say he is, then why does he need any help?"

"Well, it's a good point, but you see, it's really not help, actually. It would be having a different way to solve a problem, and no matter how good you are, whenever you got a multi-million dollar fish downhole, you're going to use every tool in the shed, and my background is a lot different than Zebb's. I came from drillings rigs and then moved over to Liner hangers and completion packers and have done a little fishing, but not near the caliber of fishing he has done. He started and stayed on workover rigs and the production side and went right into fishing tools. And, you see, Zebb is getting ready to retire in a couple years, and Bryant Harwin, the manager of Anderson Oil Tools, wants his knowledge passed on, but the only thing with ol' Zebb is he doesn't quite get along with many people, especially younger fishing hands."

"But I take it y'all get along."

"Yeah, we did some wells in Texas a ways back and we ended up on the same side, as they say." That was a short way to put it. I hoped she'd let it go at that. The last thing I wanted to do was explain how we had become friends; the fact was that he still slightly owed me.

"So take the job, what's the problem?"

"Well, I was thinking of moving on with my life and getting out of the field. It's hard to keep a girlfriend, hard to ever get married again, hard on kids once those little goblins come along—just hard on anything I ever wanted, except on the pocketbook."

She looked straight at me with a get-real smile I couldn't ignore. "Yeah, but you're not getting married anytime soon; therefore, you don't have that, and you don't have a girlfriend to worry about." She still held a smile, revealing the uncertainty of anything we might possibly have passed a first date. Not knowing fully what that meant, I let it be, hoping she was being sarcastic and that I read it right. "And if you're not getting married anytime soon, then there are no kids to worry about, or goblins as you put it, so there you have it, take the job."

I hung my head and poked at my food. "Yeah, and there never will be any kids if I get back in the oilfield. I'm twenty-eight and not getting any younger. I already got one divorce under my belt, and I'm getting a little old to continue chasing college girls."

"Yes, but you only live once. If you think you want to do it and it may set you up for the future, then go for it. Hey, you never know, a lady may not mind being an oilfield girlfriend."

"Maybe so." Most didn't mind the girlfriend part, but I racked my brain to think of one woman that truly enjoyed being an oilfield wife. The truth was that most of us were married to the rig more than we were married to the woman. Some women seemed to deal with it, but, hey, you never know, maybe there were some women out there actually thankful for the field. "I will continue my thoughts on that. Thanks for the advice."

"Well, let me know what you decide. It does sound like an opportunity though, and like you said, you're only twenty-eight, so why not? Twenty-eight is not old; you gotta live life."

"Okay." I paid the check and left a tip worthy of the wonderful service. I took my last sip of rum and thanked Sarah and Courtney for the great dinner as they wished us a nice evening and we headed out the door. I walked her to her car and made small talk about the weather, the stars, anything I could think of to get my mind off of North Dakota and anything to distract her as I slid my hand into hers. Without hesitation, her fingers grabbed mine and she squeezed my hand with a softness that broke my heart because I knew I would be leaving soon. She turned to me, her dirty blonde hair swinging over her shoulder, and I could see her small, studded diamond earring that revealed a slight sparkle. She smiled a smile that brought a sparkle to my eyes that surely must have made those diamonds envious. I guess Proverbs got it right:

> *"There are three things that are too amazing for me,*
> *four that I do not understand:*
> *The way of an eagle in the sky,*
> *The way of a snake on a rock,*
> *The way of a ship on the high seas,*
> *And the way of a man with a young woman."*
> *Proverbs 30:18-19*

CHAPTER 5

I rolled over, feeling a slight pounding in my head from the rum of the night before, and picked up the phone. "Welcome to crew change, sweetheart!" It was Bryant; I could only imagine what he wanted at six a.m.

"Thought I had a little more time than half a day. It's six a.m. How do you know I'm not nursing a hangover or got a beautiful woman in my bed?"

"Well, I know you don't have a beautiful woman in your bed—maybe a Godzilla of a woman that you thought was beautiful last night, or one of those all too common Great White Buffalo of Montana—but its seven a.m. here in Williston, and I got to have an answer. We got a job kicking off that's right up your alley, and come hell or high water, I want you on it."

"So, what you're really saying is you need an answer right now?"

"That's what I'm saying. You in or you out?"

"Damn it." I sat up in bed and leaned against the headboard, trying to collect my thoughts. "What's the pay looking like?"

"Better than frying brisket in Dillon, Montana."

"I told you yesterday, we're not frying it. It's called smoking."

"Whatever. Listen, Wyatt, the pay is good, trust me. I'll write you up an offer letter that you can sign when you get here." I knew I could trust Bryant; we had made a lot money together in North Dakota before, and he knew what it took to get a hand up there in that icebox.

"How good?"

The line went silent for a moment, and then Bryant said in a soft tone, "Twice what you were making when you left."

We had taken a pay cut by the end of the last boom, but I was still making a significant amount of money when I left. Doubling it would set me up for a long time to come. I knew I could trust him. "I'll pack up and leave first thing. See you tomorrow morning about seven."

"Sounds good."

I hung up the phone and rolled back over in bed, wondering what I had just done and wondering how I was going to tell Jessica that I wasn't going to be around for God only knew how long; then again, maybe she didn't care.

All I had seen were dollar signs and drill collars, and now I was committed. I tore through my little bit of belongings in my cramped apartment, stuffing clothes and oilfield gear into bags and boxes. I stopped for a moment and looked out the window onto Montana Street and out to the mountains and thought of the town I loved and how I would miss it. Life was peaceful around here, with no oil derricks or deadlines on the horizon.

I threw it all in the backseat of my old diesel, glanced at the frost on the windshield, and cranked up all eight cylinders. The smoke bellowed out of the exhaust, and I let the truck warm up while I gave the apartment one last scan, then locked up the rickety door, not knowing when, or if, I would be back. I didn't have much in that little apartment, a couch, a TV, and a table covered with beer bottles from previous nights. Leaving it didn't break my heart, my heart was broken long before I had moved in.

I figured I would call my landlord in a couple days and pay my fees for breaking the lease and leaving some things there; it just wasn't worth it to try and haul a bunch of secondhand furniture, and he should understand. If he didn't want to store it for me, he could have the damn furniture and the beer bottles too: either way, I was out. The time had come to get on with life.

I decided to catch breakfast at The Branding Iron on my way out of town and sadly told Courtney and Sarah that I was headed back to the field. The mood was somber as I spoke but they said they understood and wished me well. I knew I would miss this place; it was one of the reasons I moved to Dillon. Seems silly, but I couldn't find any good barbeque in Montana, until I tried this place, and it was one of the things that made me feel at home here and decide to stay. I never thought I would end up working there.

I sat down and ordered up one of their famous smoked brisket breakfast burritos mixed up with scrambled eggs and sweet potatoes. I knew what Williston had in store for breakfast entrées—$20 omelets that sucked and $10 bacon and eggs that sucked, and I was dreading every meal from here on out.

I called up my mother, who had made me promise that if I ever went back to the oilfield, I would tell her so that she could start praying once again for my safety and for the good Lord to guide me in my work. She read the papers down in Texas and knew the history of this business on account of having grown up in an oil town.

She answered with that sweet voice of a southern mother. "Hi, honey."

"Hey, Mom, how's it going down there?"

"Good. Just fixin' to head to work. What's going on?" There was no fooling her. I never called this early.

"Well, I'm headed back to the field."

The line went silent as I gave her time to soak it in. "I was wondering how long it would take for you to go back." She didn't ask why; she knew the field had adopted me ever since I had left home. It was self-explanatory. I told myself that it's all about the money, but truth be told, deep down I missed my oil family.

"Bryant called me back."

"I see; you know they are just going to burn you like they did last time." It hurt to hear, although I knew it might come true, Still, my decision had been made.

"I know, but I don't have much of a choice." I could hear her gathering things for work and a car door slam, so I assumed that she had reached the school where she worked as an interpreter for the deaf.

"What the does that mean?" I could feel her hurt and knew that I had stuck my foot right into my mouth. Truthfully, there was a choice and I had made it. "I was hoping you would come back home sometime soon."

Sarah handed me my burrito, and I nodded a thank you to her. "Mom, I really got to go. I love you."

"I love you to, son. Just be careful out there; I will be praying for you."

"Yes, ma'am."

Back in the truck after a quick breakfast, I fired the diesel up, feeling all eight cylinders pounding. I edged onto Highway 90 and put the hammer down and the engine slipped into overdrive. In my rearview, I watched the mountains and rolling hills fade behind me. It was hard leaving. I loved it here. Who could ask for more? The elk were plenty, and the people were kind.

Driving was where I did some of my best soul-searching. Maybe it was the open road or maybe it was the mundaneness of it all that freed my soul to think. As the miles rolled on, my mind jumped freely from the positives to the negatives of my decision. In what seemed like a blink, I reached Billings, sitting dead in the middle of the state. It was the line of demarcation, and I crossed it; there would be no turning back. I was returning to North Dakota like an outlaw going back to the scene of a crime. Something like destiny flitted across my mind, and I knew it was going to be a hell of run. I turned on the radio and turned it up as Jamey Johnson's classic "Lonesome Song" started playing, and the words he sang rang out: "That morning sun made its way through the windshield of my Chevrolet, whiskey eyes and ashtray breath on a chert rock gravel road. What the hell did I do last night? That's the story of my life."

Even though I didn't drive a Chevrolet, the song still hit home, and I thought about what I had done last night and about the can of worms I had opened. It was just a simple date, but it seemed like so much more. I wondered if Jessica felt the same. The song fit my soul well— lonesome—and that's probably the way it would remain. I thought about my family in Texas that I left behind almost eight years ago. After graduating high school, I had no intention of sticking around in Texas. I wanted to feel the mountains, I wanted to feel life. I wanted to feel what it was all about. I wanted to know what it was like to be a young man with nothing to lose. To leave everything comfortable, everything I knew, and just make a run for it. I wanted to live the dream. I had had nothing to lose and, to me, that was always the best time to take a leap. I prided myself on making decisions and sticking with them. I hated indecisiveness; it caused people not to trust your decision making. Most people, even if they didn't admit it, would rather you be wrong than indecisive—at least in my world, so it seemed. At least you had the balls to make a call when no one else did. Sometimes you just have to pick something and go with it whether you know if you're wrong or right; you just gotta feel it and do it. That had been one of those times, and today was one again.

I talked things over with my family before I had left Texas, and many told me I was crazy, even stupid, but I think my grandmother put it best when she said, "You're either really smart or incredibly stupid. Time will tell." Even with the success of my career, I'm still not sure which one of those are true of myself. I had nothing to lose back then; it was great. It's so much easier to make decisions when you have nothing to lose. Sometimes I missed those times. My decisions now always seemed to have something riding on them—somebody's life, either physical or financial, or just their well-being. Sometimes I missed the times of not having responsibilities. I knew now how those oilfield old timers felt when they used to tell me that they wished they had their first green hardhat back. I used to ask why. I couldn't understand why they would want to be the newest, dumbest, and lowest paid, but now I got it. It came down to two words: responsibility sucks. Besides, it's pretty hard to get fired when you don't know anything. They don't expect much; therefore, you just did what they asked, and that was that.

I remember talking over the adventure of going to

Wyoming to work gas wells many nights with my high school fiancé, debating about what we would do when we graduated, and she was highly in favor of heading up to Wyoming, mostly because we were on the run because of her being 17 and taking up with me. The pay would be good, and the dream was even better, even if we didn't know what that dream really held. I knew it would have to be better, and at the very least, I would have a story to tell. I figured it was worth the risk and packed my bags in the same old diesel that I was driving today and, as they say, "Headed west." That sun really did hit that windshield on that trip, and lonesome ran deep in our bones as we left everything and everybody we had ever known. I said my prayers the whole way there, hoped for the best, and trusted that God would help me not fall flat on my face, and if I did, it must be the best for me. The rest is history, as Jessica had said.

....

I pulled into the sleepy town of Williston, North Dakota, at around one a.m. The town had grown and was much more active than I remembered it being. I saw that National Oilwell Varco had started on a new shop bigger than the first and larger than the one downtown, and I took note of the latest expansion from Halliburton and wondered what they knew that I didn't. I knew that the call from Bryant hadn't come lightly; he had some of the best fishing/completion hands in the business, and he himself was no slacker. It seemed that everybody was gearing up.

I drove to the only twenty-four hour restaurant, Lonnie's Truck Stop. I was due for a pit stop and wanted to stretch my legs before signing into a hotel. I pulled around front and couldn't find a parking spot. Strange. There was hardly anybody here the last time I was in town at this hour. I was just glad they were open. I pulled around back and found a spot next to a grease-laden dumpster and made my way inside to a booth.

The waitress licked her pencil and pulled her pad out. "Whatta you want?" She didn't seem to care much about being friendly; probably being jilted one too many times by a trucker gave her that cold demeanor.

"Pigs in a blanket." Sausage wrapped in pancakes sounded delicious, even with an unfriendly waitress writing my order. I hadn't eaten since breakfast in Dillon and regretted waiting so long. "And a cup of decaf," I added. She didn't say anything, just turned and walked off and put the order in. I wondered what her deal was, she was sure no Sarah. I scoped the place out and watched her take another order. I realized that she and a couple of other waitresses were the only females in the joint. The place sat full of truck drivers and rig hands who couldn't sleep while waiting on their shift.

There was a guy wearing a trench coat who kept walking past me while bobbing his head to the beat of the music his headphones pounded in his ears. I wondered if he was meth'd out because he seemed to have no sense of boundaries, and his focus was purely set on roaming back and forth in the restaurant. He walked within inches of my table while staring down at me, fully invading my space. I stared back with a confused look, pondering what in the hell this guy's deal was. I didn't say anything to him because I figured he was expecting me to, but his stare creeped me out to no end. When he stopped beside my table, I wished I had carried my Glock in with me, but I hadn't even thought about it. I was too used to Montana, there was no need to carry all the time.

This guy, though, gave me a spooky feeling. I was in a bad spot, sitting there waiting to be pounced on while his head continued that strange bob in rhythm to the music I heard escaping his headphones. He stood over six feet tall and had about 75 pounds on me. I wondered what he had under the coat, and the thought crossed my mind to punch him straight in the gut and then bury my head in his chest as I charged him in order to knock him onto a table. If all went as I planned, I would then be able to pound his face until he begged for mercy, which I hoped I wouldn't hear because I would have grabbed a hold of his throat. I wanted the first punch, the first hit, and I wanted it to be vicious. I didn't know why my blood was starting to boil, but my senses were tingling nonetheless.

"Can you move?" I heard my waitress snap at the back of his head. I watched as she impatiently waited for the giant to lumber out of the way. He suddenly snapped back into reality and continued out the front door, once again bobbing his head to the beat of his music. She sat my coffee down with a thud; some of it splashed over the top.

"He was quite strange," I said.

She looked at me, surprised that I seemed shocked. "Everybody in here is strange these days." With that, she turned away, and my thoughts wandered as I waited for my food. I couldn't get my mind off of Jessica for the last couple hours of the trip. I thought of calling her but also dreaded the idea. I didn't want a conversation that might end in goodbye; I wanted to dream just for a little bit; I wanted it all to be right a little bit longer. There was no fighting the fact that she was heavy on my mind. It weighed on me wondering how she would feel about dating a divorced man. I ate my pigs, once delivered, and left with the thought of that creep waiting for me out back by the dumpster, but he wasn't, and I was glad for it. I never saw him again, but I swore that in the future I wouldn't hang out around this town at one a.m. This wasn't the Williston I remembered, and I wondered just how bad it had become.

I drove back into the main part of town that I had passed on Highway 2 while headed to Lonnie's and found a place to make my living quarters, if that's what you wanted to call it. It was the Airport International Inn. I always wondered why they gave it the International name; they named the place as if Asian millionaires were flying in daily. I guess I couldn't blame them for trying. There was a vibe in the town that hadn't been here before, though. I don't know if it was my oilfield roots or a change in the weather, but I could feel something in this town, something big, something definitely different.

I caught the last room available for rent and paid my $200 fee, still laughing to myself about the name and shaking my ahead about the cost, holding tight to my receipt keeping a mental note to turn it in for expenses. I walked down the hall and slid the keycard into the electronic lock. The room left a lot to be desired. The bed was made, but it appeared haphazard, and I could tell that the sheets under the bedspread were wrinkled. In the bathroom, there were remnants of somebody's hair that lingered in the sink as if someone had just put down the razor. I glanced over and was disgusted to see urine still covering the floor. In any other town, I would have demanded my money back, but there was nowhere else to stay in Williston. I had already called around on my way in, and there was nothing. I thought about sleeping in my truck, but that frightened me more than someone's urine. There was little doubt in my mind that I would be staying here tomorrow night, though. There had to be something else. I placed clean sheets from the closet on the bed and laid my body to rest as my eyelids closed down along with my mind.

"Mmm." The low murmur of a throaty, feminine groan.

"Nnngh!" A distinct grunt, this time a man's.

"Ah ... uh!" The female voice again.

"Mmph!" The sound of the man's voice, reciprocating.

"Uuuuuh!" The female voice, louder and more intense.

It took a second to realize what I was hearing, but the pounding against the thin-walled sheetrock behind my headboard as the chorus of moans and yelps echoed on the other side of the wall answered all my questions. Normally, the obvious coupling on the other side of the wall wouldn't have upset me. You couldn't hold anything against love, but I just wanted to sleep. It was closing in on two a.m. Couldn't they have gotten this over with around 10 o'clock and gone to sleep like normal people do?

"Trying to sleep over here!" I banged on the wall, but all I heard was their laughter and more forceful pounding that continued to drone on. I tore the covers off and placed my head at the foot of the bed and tried to find some sort of rest, to no avail. I lay there until six a.m., finally getting out of bed without feeling very rested. As I exited the room, I took note of a man who was knocking on the door of the room that kept me up all night, and I saw a beautiful brunette open the door and pull him to the room. As he entered, she glanced out of her doorway at me with a smile on her face and an inviting raise of eyebrows as her tongue found its way across her top lip. Disgusted and disturbed, I wondered what had happened to the sleepy little town I had left only a couple of years ago.

CHAPTER 6

I made my way to the front door of Anderson Oil Tools shop with the wind gusting against me head on while I fought the chill of a North Dakota fall. The thermometer that hung outside the shop read 30 degrees. That wasn't bad except for the wind that iced my bones. Western Montana was cold, but at least the mountains blocked a lot of the wind. Here, I could feel the bitterness on my bare hands from forgetting my gloves in the truck, and I hurried into the side door to find Bryant and some warmth.

The inside of the shop was nothing special—pretty standard white walls with some green trim. Two bays and a concrete floor. Nevertheless, I knew the jobs we could run out of a small shop, and it was a sure thing that we would push this shop to the limit. I looked around and saw Bryant zealously inspecting a rack of packers and verifying some parts, just as I expected him to be at 7 a.m., overanxious and overeager to get started. I waited, not wanting to interrupt, and poured a cup of coffee from the pot in the back sitting next to the wash-up sink, which I doubted would actually pass a health inspection. I really was in no hurry, even if he was; there was still a groove I had to get in. I had just driven a good 10 hours to this Artic fall-weather town they called Williston. I sipped my coffee, noticing the familiar Folger's bitterness that I couldn't complain about because it hit the spot, especially with the lack of sleep I was suffering from. A little java in the morning was just what I needed.

I made small talk with the shop crew as they sneaked

over for a fresh cup. Nobody was feeling that ambitious except for Bryant, apparently. He and I had ended up together on a couple of jobs over the last couple of years and had evidently rubbed off on one another. We did some pretty difficult jobs and solved many wellbore issues. He was quite well-versed in his skills and was playing the role of the Fishing Manager right now, overseeing multiple jobs and several field hands like myself. Fishing jobs included retrieving stuck pipe and fishing out dropped pipe, along with getting packers out of the hole—all tasks that required more than a little finesse. I, on the other hand, had a knack for setting packers and getting them out of the hole, and while these two professions go hand in hand, a lot of time they can be quite a bit different on approaches to the same problem, although they both have to figure out the right tool to run due to wellbore conditions. Traditionally, packer hands deal with more of the fluid and mathematics that affect wellbores, and fishing hands like to grab ahold of something in whatever way possible and beat it out of the well—in whatever way seems effective. It's all about choosing the right hook and the right bait to get that fish to bite. If all else fails—mill it up.

There has been a long rivalry between fishing hands and packer hands for many years due to the fact that they can face the same problem and have two very different solutions that both work, but the fishing hand, for whatever reason, walks off with twice as much money, wrong or right.

"How's it going, Bryant?" I asked between a sip of joe and shook his hand. Bryant was a hell of guy, on the downside of his prime at just under 40, but still in it. He was one of those managers who, as long as you remained an effective hand, would look after you the way a big brother would. He had your best interests at heart, and you could trust that. He had some years on him, but the drive was not gone.

"Business is good, oil prices are edging up, and I haven't slept in three days. Times are good." He poured himself a cup and took a soothing sip, and I could see the bags under his eyes.

"You think you could at least have some halfway decent coffee. I know it's been a hard last couple of years, but for Pete's sake, a guy still has to live a little."

"Yeah, I know. It's what the shop likes, though, and it gets the job done."

He looked worn out. I asked how his family was and how they were holding up in Williston. He said they were good, but I knew he was looking for a way out if it ever presented itself. Nobody wanted to stay in Williston long term. Finally, he said, "All right, down to business. Let's go upstairs; we got a well drawing up there."

My Redwings pounded the steel stairs rising from the shop to the offices upstairs as I followed Bryant up, and he led me to a large room with a white board up front and a large round table set up as though expecting King Arthur. This was where it all went down; you could tell this was a decision-making room. Every fishing tool company has one, a room that you can bring oil executives and consultants into, and everybody puts their heads together while they have Houston or Denver on speaker from the receiver in the middle of the table, but this wasn't one of those jobs, at least not yet. The room was empty, and I was glad to see it. I looked at the well drawing—as I had many times before when analyzing surveys—that was taped up with real professional gray duct tape on the white board. I noticed some tight spots where we would be working and a horizontal section of the well at an 87-degree angle, which indicated that we'd be well below the Liner Top that hung the entire horizontal casing section. I looked over it thoroughly as Bryant gave me a second to soak it up, and I jotted notes for later reference in my tally book.

There was always something missing when dealing with the underworld of downhole; somebody always seems to hide something. The drawing simply didn't tell all the details, but it was a start. When it's all you got, it's all you've got, and it's about as close as you're ever going to get to being able to see down that hole, and you have to make it work. Some people don't realize how a small detail can change a wellbore fishing plan. One-sixteenth of an inch can save a company thousands or cost it millions. I always tried to pay very close attention to how large the inner diameter of the casing was— down to the hundredths of an inch—and note if there were any restrictions because the last thing you want is to be downhole with a tool too large and make a mess or waste an oil company's time, or worst of all, look like a moron, or as they like to say in the industry, "Worm out." The depth of the Liner hanger that Bryant pointed out to me was at 9100 feet on the nuts, and that was the end of the vertical section of the well and the end of the larger size casing, the seven-inch portion of the well. The Liner hanger was a very pivotal part of the well. It began the start of a smaller section of basing below it—the four-and-a-half-inch section. This smaller section was the horizontal section; in the picture, it looked as if it was a very long foot, with the vertical section resembling the leg and the horizontal section resembling the foot. He pointed to the diagram and informed me of the situation they were having as I listened.

"They had just set their Liner hanger and had gotten a severe increase in pressure while they were pulling out of the hole. Everything was successful on their Liner hanger set, and they were able to get a solid test to three-thousand psi after the set. So, everything is good there. The problem is, of course, all this pressure they are dealing with now, and where it's coming from. Obviously, there is a hole somewhere in the casing, but they don't know where, and they want to find it ASAP. So that's where you come in, Wyatt. The debate right now is which packer to run—the large one that you set up above the Liner Top to test, or the small one that you can get below the Liner Top so that you can test below it."

I mulled it over and spoke up. "I'm thinking we run the larger one with a smaller plug below it to be set below Liner Top. Even if that Liner Top held at three-thousand psi, the weakest link is still the Liner hanger. The fact that it was just set and that's what changed in the well bore means I think we need to test it and make sure it's good."

"That's my thoughts too. The problem is going to be convincing Rikki, the oil consultant, to let us run it."

"He's one of those guys, huh?" I always loved the guys that call you to fix their problems but tell you how you're going to do it. I mean, it makes sense, doesn't it? Your house has a leak somewhere you can't see and is filling the basement with water, so you call the plumber. When the plumber gets there, you tell him you know right where the leak is and how to fix it. It always puts you in a pickle, but that's just business as usual. You have to know the game to play so that it puts the odds in your favor with customers like this; sometimes you just have to let the customer be stupid and deposit money in your pocket.

Bryant stood with his arms folded, thinking on the situation. "Yes, indeed. He is one of those guys. Why don't you just take both packers, big and small, out to location and hash it out there? You will, of course, need a plug that you will be running below that packer in order to test against it. One other thing: you had better button up; it's supposed to get chilly."

"Sure thing. It's always chilly in this state. What makes today any different?" He laughed at the truth of it and took a final sip of his coffee. "I'll get loaded up." He threw me the keys and told me to go find the truck out front.

I zipped up my Carharrt duck coat, pulled my beanie out from my back pocket, and fitted it over my noggin. Chilly is a constant state in North Dakota, especially in October. This area can just flat-out suck to work in, no doubt about it, but at the same time I preferred it over the Middle East any day of the week. It's common knowledge that God put oil in the most godforsaken parts of the world. Wherever oil is, I can guarantee you that people don't want to be there, unless, of course, you pay them very well. That thought reminded me that I still needed to sign the papers with Bryant about my pay; I was curious to find out what my windfall was going to amount to, but because of the gravity of the situation, I figured we could do it a little later.

I went out to the parking lot and clicked the alarm button in order to find my truck. I heard an annoying blast of BEEP! BEEP! BEEP! and was surprised by what the alarm was coming from. I had expected a run-down truck with a 100,000 miles on it, definitely 50,000, but instead there was a brand new, silver 2010 Dodge Ram 4-door 2500. It was beautiful and fully loaded, sporting a long bed and tinted windows along with nerf bars on the side to make getting in easy. I felt a little spoiled and undeserving, but I knew this truck came with many expectations. Number one, go make Anderson Oil Tools some money to pay for it. I have to say they did me right on the truck; maybe this gig wouldn't be so bad after all.

It had, in fact, gotten chillier during our little 30-minute meeting. The thermometer outside had now settled at 22 degrees; it had dropped 8 degrees in 30 minutes, even though the sun had come up. I was just glad it was above zero, but Lord only knew how long it would stay that way. I felt the chill wrap around my cheeks as my face reddened from it. The cold wouldn't have had near the bite if it weren't for the wind. The wind always seemed to make everything ten times colder. I slipped into my truck and felt the icy cold of the leather creep through my jeans. I immediately punched on the seat heater. Before nightfall, I was going to need long johns. Hopefully, it would warm up when that sun got a little higher in the sky, but it didn't look promising. I already had big plans for this truck's future. I saw myself in the very near future putting in a remote start and billing it to Anderson Oil Tools on the grounds of I didn't want to be cold any longer than I had to be.

I pulled onto Highway 2 and headed toward Tioga, which awaited me 45 miles east. I slowed to the glow of brake lights up ahead and slid to a stop, feeling the ice below my own tires, and looked beyond the fifteen cars sitting at a stop in front of me. Three cars had skidded off the highway; two were in the ditch and one had been T-boned by another. I hoped no one was hurt. I wasn't going anywhere anytime soon, and made the decision to dial up the number Bryant had given me for Rikki, the customer waiting on me out at the site.

The ring sounded and a gruff voice came over the line: "Hello."

"This is Wyatt, with Anderson Oil Tools, and I wanted to let you know I'm stuck behind a wreck with a couple of cars in the ditch."

"How long before you think you're here?"

"At least an hour and a half, maybe two with the roads how they are and waiting for them to clear these guys out of my way." It was not the response I wanted to give and definitely not the response he wanted to hear, but it was the truth nonetheless.

"Hurry every chance you get. We're waiting on you." I heard silence from the dead phone on the other end. I took the phone from my ear and looked at it as if it had just betrayed me. What a prick! He probably didn't grow up on cornbread and brisket with an attitude like that. If this is how he handled something minor that couldn't be avoided, I would hate to see how he reacted when something major happened or, even worse, when something happened that could have been avoided.

....

While looking up at the idle 120-ft. tall drilling rig, I pulled across the cattle guard onto location. Snow was starting to pack up around the buildings outside of the rig. I saw no movement, which probably meant everyone was waiting on me. My stomach sank because I hated to make any company wait. I backed my truck up next to the largest shack, where I expected to find Rikki, the man in charge, the man who the oil company hired to control the well, the man who hired me to work on this well, and THE MAN who held all the cards, or so such people liked to think. Many of the oil consultants thought they were gods out here, which was laughable. Still, at the end of the day, even though he put his pants on one leg at a time, he did reserve the right to run me off location.

I knocked on the door of his trailer, which could have passed for an upper-class single-wide, and entered. Long, fake-looking granite counter tops covered the length of the trailer, and the windows looked out toward the rig. Four rig monitors were situated atop the long counter; it sort of resembled a stock trader's office. This was where everything was tracked; you could tell a tank's volume from across location if you chose to do so. Rikki sat behind the desk, and I made a quick appraisal. He was short and plump; I could tell that even though he was sitting down. I guessed he was close to 5' 8"; he sported a full beard, and clean blue overalls covered his large frame. He probably looked awkward in regular dress pants or probably couldn't find any to fit him. His swollen belly limited how close he could draw up to his desk, and he didn't seem too ambitious about getting up to greet me or about anything else for that matter. I excused it and didn't much care; after all, nobody wants to see a packer hand, and definitely not one trained as a fisherman; we only show up when the well is at its worst.

"Took me a little longer to get here than I would have liked, but I made it; roads were extremely icy."

"Yeah, I figured they would be. First ice of the season. Ain't it fucking great?" He looked me over from head to toe. "How old are you?"

"Thirty-two." I always lied about my age on location; it was habit. I was only 28, but he didn't need to know that.

"Hmm," he scoffed. "Your daddy let you come out and play?"

"Look, if you want to measure the wrinkles on my balls, we can do that, but if you want this job done, then I'm your guy, so you take your pick."

He smiled at the retort and gave a brief chuckle. First rule of oil field politics, take no prisoners. I silently waited for him to either run me off or agree with me.

"All right. What do you wanna do here, son?"

I stepped closer to him, placing my open tally book on his desk. He looked it over while I gestured at the sketch and laid out my plan. "I was going to run the seven-inch packer, due to the fact that a lot of the times the leak is still at the Liner Top because when they set them, you can only take it to about three thousand psi and check the tool; whereas with a packer in the hole, we can go up to ten thousand psi if we want to and isolate it. We have to face the fact that the Liner Top is the weakest link in the well bore at this time."

"We're not running in and testing something that has already been tested. It's a fucking waste of time."

I picked up my tally book, folded it, and gave a terse reply. "Well, I guess that settles it. We'll run in with the four-and-a-half packer and run it below the Liner Top." There was no use in arguing, it was his well after all. He had only hired me to fix it, asked for my opinion, and then ignored my suggestions. He really just wanted me to put tools down the well. So, that's what he was going to get.

I put my tool measurements on the desk for him to go over and tally up himself if he desired and walked out, letting him know I would get tools picked up right away and started downhole. I was glad to be back; it could be a strange world at times, but one that I found fitted me quite well.

I backed the truck in as a worn-in roughneck guided

me to the catwalk that sat out in front of the drilling rig. I watched closely so as not to run him over. He stopped me just a few feet short of the catwalk. I always thought it was funny that they called it a catwalk and nobody quite knew where it came from. It was essentially a huge chunk of steel laid out in a section 10-ft. wide and 45-ft. long with a slide that went up to the floor to be used to lay down tools or pick them up. The modeling industry has theirs and we have ours, and, in fact, they weren't a whole lot different except that one is made of metal and has bearded oily guys walking on it with tools, and the other has models strutting new clothing for Calvin Klein. What most likely happened was that a bunch of roughnecks were sitting around while drilling and lusting over models at the same time that they were trying to name equipment, and "catwalk" is what they came up with—at least, I could see it happening that way. Regardless, I jumped in the back of the Dodge and unstrapped my tools and dragged them out onto the catwalk and instructed the roughneck to give me a hand. We dragged my packer and plug out of the truck and placed them on the catwalk. I looked over and saw a circle of roughnecks just watching us, talking about only God knows what, but the fact that they were watching and not helping gave me a pretty good indication of the greenness of their crew. It was worth keeping in the back of my mind because if things got out of hand, I knew I couldn't trust them and needed to stay on my toes when we got up to the floor.

"Tell your buddies that instead of sitting around holding each other's hand, they can go up to the floor and start pulling these tools up," I said to the roughneck who had actually been helping me.

"Okay. Will do." He didn't argue, which surprised me;

he just needed a little direction. He probably wasn't very familiar with a tool hand being on site. All he knew was that I was clean and had just come out of that consultant's shack, so I must at least be somewhat in charge, and that was good enough for him, I suppose.

They started to send the winch line down while I finished up a couple of measurements and instructed them on how I wanted my tools to be picked up. I always liked picking up the packer first, then the plug second because the plug will go underneath, and it's easier to deal with it that way on the floor. I choked the strap around my tools, pulling it tight as I hooked up the winch line. I threw my index finger in the air to motion for them to start hoisting, and as they did, I guided the tools up the beaver slide that connected from the catwalk up to the rig floor. I instructed the hand who was still beside me and had watched me to do the same with the plug and retrieving head that lay on the catwalk.

I quickly began climbing up the stairs double fast in order to beat my tools up to the floor and in order to diffuse any confusion that their arrival might create with the hands up top, which was warranted because drilling hands really didn't see these tools often, if ever. These were tools they used on the production side more than on the drilling side and were much different from what a rig hand used.

I noticed the driller standing with his hand wrapped around the brake handle controlling the whole rig by the steel in his hand. He was a young guy, probably older than me but not by much. He stood just slightly above eye level to me and sported a full beard with grease that seemed to be kneaded in. He wore no safety glasses, just blue jeans and a long-sleeve, dark blue work shirt. Being a driller gave him the right to have a heater right next to him, which was the greatest of luxuries in cold country. Maybe it was my Texas blood, but I felt everyone should have their own personal heater. If it were up to me, I would enclose the whole damn rig.

"I'm Vann. Good to meet you." He shook my hand and seemed to have ambitions of squeezing it off.

"You too, the name is Wyatt. " I returned the high pressure squeeze. "We need to pick up three hundred feet of 2 7/8 tubing to run up above of our packer so we can get these tools below Liner Top."

"Will do boss."

We swung the packer that was still hanging on the winch line over to the middle of the floor as I yelled to one of the roughnecks to slap the hole cover on and put a coco mat down, and we stabbed the packer down on top of the mat while three of us held it. One hand stood on a ladder turning the tubing with a 24" pipe wrench as we finagled the packer, trying to get the threads to line up and screw together; we looked like four monkeys trying to figure out what to do with a football. I felt the threads start to catch and got a couple of threads going and then got Vann to pick up on the string, which allowed us to screw the packer on easier.

Many people get confused when you start talking about packer work and definitely get confused when you start explaining fishing work. The fact is that I haven't seen another industry do anything remotely similar. I don't know anyone who knows anyone that can really relate to it outside the oilfield. Packers really are not that confusing; although there are many different models that function differently, all the basics are the same. A packer is about 7 feet in length and is a piece of iron that is small enough to go into a casing. It has a setting mechanism of sorts that allows you to energize three rubber packing elements on the outside of the packer that seal against the casing walls; in turn, fluid can then pump through the packer and below the packing elements while no fluid is going above the elements. A packer is very essential to getting fluid where it needs to be, whether it is cement, acid, water, or drill fluid, because you can't just start pumping cement and expect things to work out. It just doesn't happen; you will end up with 10,000 feet of fence post. In the case of an oil well, to find a leak in the casing, a packer is essential to isolating certain sections. The thing to remember is that a packer is a tool— as a wrench is to a mechanic, a packer is to a tool hand. The well bore is the problem, so understanding the tool is the easy part, but understanding the well, that's a completely different story.

The crew did well getting the packer screwed on and helping me stab an 8-ft. pup joint below the packer with the retrieving head for the plug. The retrieving head would just latch right up to the plug and carry it downhole until I manipulated it enough to get it off the plug so that I could move my packer up hole and start isolating. We stabbed the retrieving head onto the plug and picked it up in order to verify that everything looked good. I took one last look as we tightened up connections and double-checked elements for any deformities and a couple of serial numbers.

"You going to spit on that?" Vann hollered as he waited on my decision. There was no doubt about that; I hocked the biggest loogie I could muster and bent down to the very bottom of my tools and spit it out, and just as soon as the saliva left my lips, two other roughnecks—Dakotah, a very large Sioux, and Jeff, a wiry young fellow—bent down and hocked their biggest onto the elements of the packer as well. It was an old-time tradition, a superstition at its finest, especially on drilling rigs. One very rarely if ever let tools go downhole without being spat on. Nobody has any clue where it started, but it was here to stay and would probably last forever in the oilfield. Vann nodded as if we had just sincerely accomplished something, and I held the tools as steady as possible and motioned for him to lower them downhole as we started the journey downhole that we like to call a "trip."

We put the 10 joints of tubing on top of the packer, and I took a mental note that we only had about 300 feet of testing we could do before the drill pipe ran into the Liner Top and got stuck, which would be an absolute nightmare. Three hundred feet was all we needed because they had sleeves down past that, and I didn't want to get anywhere near them. If that's where the leak was, it was a whole other set of problems.

I walked back downstairs and felt the wind whip my face as the snow shoved itself down my coat, which reminded me to dig out my hardhat liner as soon as I got back to my truck. My idea was to let the rig do its thing and get us down close to the Liner Top. There was no need to sit up there and baby sit; I had already let 'em know to run her easy and come and get me if they had any problems.

I sat in my truck and sipping my coffee as I let the warmth soak through my bones; it was still Folger's, though, there was no changing that. I took out my well drawing that I had made back at the shop with Bryant and drew a separation where the Liner Top would be and wrote 9100 beside it to remember to look out for it and get the right joint count as they were tripping in the hole. Sometimes it could be a real doozy to get through Liner Tops with these tools cause the well necks down at Liner Top, but I hoped they would slide right in. We would soon find out.

CHAPTER 7

I glanced up toward the rig floor as I noticed drops of oil landing on my windshield. Puzzled, I watched through the rain drops of oil starting to gain rapidly onto my windshield as Dakotah's large Sioux frame raced up the stairs leading to the rig floor, his feet only touching every other stair. I stepped out of the warmth of the cab, slapped my hardhat on top of my skull, and raced toward the same stair case Dakotah had just soared up.

"Stab that TIW!" Vann screamed out to Dakotah and me as he manipulated drilling controls. Dakotah was trying to manhandle the oversized TIW safety valve. As I caught sight of the closed position of the valve he lifted, I quickly scrambled to find the wrench to open the valve, which was always supposed to stay open in case this scenario ever happened. It doesn't work very well to stab a closed valve because the pressure will force against the valve and you might never be able to stab it and get it shut.

"We haven't been able to find it anywhere!" hollered Vann as he realized what I was looking for. He left the controls, joining me as we scoured the rig floor.

I darted over to the job box and threw the lid open, hoping that it didn't come back on top of my head as I dug around for a huge Allen wrench that would work.

"Found it!" I screamed out toward Vann as I raced over and opened the valve; oil continued spewing out of the drill pipe, drenching through my overalls with my skin starting to feel the slime of Bakken crude. Vann, Dakotah, and I grabbed the safety valve, trying to hold it down as oil continued furiously spewing up through it. I felt a thread grab as we furiously spun the valve deeper into the connection. I grabbed the wrench and snugged it tight into the fitting and turned, shutting the oil off from down below. I looked over at Dakotah, who was gasping for breath and leaning against the A-leg of the derrick in disbelief.

"This battle ain't over, Sally. Get up and get that backside closed in or you're going to have the same thing there!" You could tell from the tone in Vann's voice that he meant business. It was true. That backside needed to be shut off immediately, and I was glad Vann was on the same page as me; most of all, I was glad Rikki hadn't made it up to the floor yet.

I couldn't believe the amount of pressure we were getting in a supposedly cased hole well—definitely a good indication that something was seriously wrong down there.

I felt the slime of oil dripping down my back as I realized I was soaked from head to toe in the green goo of the Bakken. I looked over at Vann, who was wetter than I was and who had oil dripping off his beard. "You gonna get some heavier fluid in that well, Vann?" I asked.

He glanced over at me knowingly. "Just as soon as I can get that derrick hand on the pits to send me some heavy mud." Again, we were thinking on the same page.

"How heavy you got?"

"Heaviest now is eleven point six pounds per gallon." I knew 11.6 pounds probably wouldn't be enough, but if it's all we had, then it's all we had.

"While we're waiting, as soon as we get her shut in, let's get a shut-in pressure."

"Okay." There was no question we were working together on this; it was standard operating procedure to see the pressure you were dealing with in order to know how heavy your fluid needed to be.

I watched as oil dripped from Vann's hand onto the phone receiver that reached the entire rig by megaphone. "Motor man, I need the annular rubber closed immediately." At the same time, I noticed the worst of sights—Rikki starting to hobble out of his shack while still zipping up his coveralls and holding a stainless steel coffee cup. He was scurrying his worried self up to the rig floor in short time, at least for an oversized feller. I was just glad he wasn't up here to find out they had had a closed TIW valve on the floor along with no wrench nearby. How that happened, I wasn't sure, but I imagined that Vann would be having a discussion with the crew at the end of this tour. At least I hoped.

Rikki walked onto the floor, glanced around at the oil dripping off every A-leg of the derrick and down to an oil-slicked iron floor, and looked at us. "Vann, what the hell happened?"

"Don't know, boss. It just came from nowhere."

"Wyatt, how close are we to the Liner Top and getting to set that plug and packer?"

"We are five hundred feet away from the Liner Top and eight hundred feet away from getting a set."

"Damn it." I knew what he was after, which was to get down there and set that plug and seal everything off, but if the leak was not below the Liner Top, this plug would do us absolutely no good. It sure would have been a good time to have the larger packer in the hole because we could set sooner and gain control closing off the pressure below us, but it was definitely not a good time to remind him of that.

"Either way, we got to get this well killed before we do anything," I muttered.

Rikki crossed his arms and spoke up again; I could see veins starting to poke out from the fat on his forehead. "Yeah, I know. I was just hoping we were closer than that." I really didn't know what to tell him because it was irrelevant to what he was hoping.

He looked at me with uncertainty. "You got this under control, Wyatt? I got to head back down to make some phone calls"

"We're good here. Do your thing."

Vann looked over at me as we watched the oversized blue leprechaun disappear down the stairs. As he walked away, Vann quietly leaned over to me and muttered, "You think he would have stuck around a little longer since we just about lost the damn well."

"That's why he makes the big bucks," I said sarcastically. Vann laughed; comedy in a situation like this wasn't always bad.

We heard the intercom from inside the doghouse as the derrick hand came over the phone. "We got a tank full of eleven point six pound mud."

Vann went over to his receiver, "Copy that. Give me just a second to get these pressures, and I'll have you send it down."

The voice came back, "Copy, Drill."

We looked over to see if the casing pressure had stabilized and it had, at 1800 psi, which was a good kick, and the drill pipe pressure was sitting steady at 2100 psi.

"Send that 11.6 down," I told Vann.

"How much?"

"As much as you got. Let's get that whole well bore full of it, if possible."

"Copy."

I took a seat on the bench to take a load off and to contemplate the situation. Everything Vann had ordered was spot on, and I couldn't have done any better, nor did I know anyone that could've. I looked over at him. "You know that's not heavy enough to kill this…" I didn't want to insult him, and I figured he knew it wouldn't kill this kick, but we had to get it out in the open.

"Yep, sure do. But when it's all you got, it's all you got."

"Very true. We are definitely going to need to weight up, no doubt about it." Most people get confused when you speak about weighting up, at least those that don't make their living in the oil patch, but it was really simple. You add barite to your drilling mud, which makes your fluid a heavier weight, which in turn puts more hydrostatic pressure onto the pressure that is coming up from the well bore in order to kill that wellbore pressure so you can work without your head being blown off.

He grabbed a calculator that sat on the steel of the knowledge box that held every well control manual you could image along with any other knowledge needed, and pounded in some numbers as he took a deep breath. "Yep. No doubt about that." He hadn't done the math until now; he hadn't had time. The man was trying to get this well under control and was doing an excellent job. It reminded me of what I missed about not being on a drilling rig. This was the stuff we lived for, got paid for, were made for. It was a rush, one of a kind and all its own.

I walked over to the side of the rig and looked out. I could see every hand scrambling to check on things. A casual observer would have seen chaos, but I knew we were going to gain control of this well as long as every one of us worked together and as long as we stayed on our toes.

We needed the whole system to be at least 12.5 pounds, in and out. With a kick this size, I didn't want to mess around with it. It had the potential to take us all out, and I wanted heavier mud in the system if at all possible. It really wasn't my job to deal with this; I was here to set a packer and get a test and try to find a hole, but as I looked around for Rikki, he was nowhere to be seen, and he didn't seem to care if we lost control of it, and apparently he had delegated it to me and Vann, which was probably better for the oil company anyway.

Vann finished his numbers and grabbed the oil slathered receiver that dripped Bakken crude. "Derrick hand, pick up!" His icy tone meant business and you could hear it throughout the entire rig on the intercom.

No answer.

"Derrick hand, pick up the fucking phone!"

"Yes, Drill?"

"What the fuck were you doing?"

"Bringing a load of bar over."

I watched as Vann's face relaxed. "Good! Get that shit in the hole!"

The true name of bar was actually barite, but nobody called it that except geologists and miners. Barite is a dense sulfate mineral that can occur in a variety of rocks, including limestone and sandstone, with a range of accessory minerals, such as quartz, chert, dolomite, calcite, siderite, and metal sulfides. We used it in situations like this to weight up the system, to keep that kick from the well bore from blowing us to the moon.

Vann looked over at me and shrugged. "Maybe I was a little rough on him."

"Ah, it's good for 'em. I wouldn't sweat it."

"Kind of hard to be mad at him when he was doing what I was thinking." I laughed as I sat on the bench wishing I had a cup of coffee to ease my nerves and to scratch the itch to have a drink in my hand. It was always funny to me how when you get a crew that's been together for a while, they become like brothers, and some more like twins. You begin to read each other's mind on what's to happen next—you just get used to each other. My old driller Jeremiah got legitimately pissed at me one time for not reading his mind. I remember looking at him with my head cocked to my shoulder in disbelief like a confused dog. He apologized, but, nevertheless, that's what was expected.

I continued imagining that cup of coffee, a comforting thought, as I walked over to look at the shut-in pressures. Thankfully, they were staying the same, and I pondered what exactly might be going on down there. It really didn't make sense. They had just landed their Liner, and everything was tested. There was no open hole exposed, which meant there was no reason to see this kind of pressure, but, regardless, it was there, and it was my problem.

I walked back into the doghouse and let Vann know I was going down to the pits to check on the guys and see how they were doing. He couldn't leave; someone had to stay up there in case things changed, and he was the man for the job.

I walked the pits, glancing through the grates and noticing the agitators turning and mixing the invert and barite, prepping it to be sent downhole. I made my way below to the hopper house where I saw what looked like an oversized 300-pound ghost wearing a hard hat throwing 100 pound sacks of bar from a pallet on to the hopper. To inject into the system, you had to insert barite over time. Too much at one time and it wouldn't get distributed through the tank and would just be compacted powder lying on the bottom. He was breathing heavily as he rested on the hopper stand holding the last sack of bar he tossed. He sliced the bag down the center and eased it into the hopper as it injected into the mud system to get mixed; the bar powder covered him from head to toe, and he was moving as fast as he could muster, trying to get the system weighed up while catching his breath.

"You want me to get you one of those floor hands?" I yelled over the hum of a centrifugal pump inside the hopper house.

"I'm good!" he yelled back.

"Well, not good enough! I'm getting a hand over here to help." He acted insulted, but sympathy had escaped me; it was true, he needed a hand. The simple fact was that there was no possibility of him weighting up too fast, and he was getting whipped from throwing 100-pound sacks.

It was a short walk up to the shakers. I felt the drum of the vibrations from all three shakers buzz through me, even though there was no fluid moving across them since we were shut in. That was their job, to shake everything out except the fluid we wanted to keep by using screens that fluid would fall through back into the mud system and small vibration motors to make it shake. I noted the two floor hands standing around looking at blank shale screens, waiting. "One of you guys needs to get down there and help that derrick hand throw sacks. I don't care which one. Preferably the one who doesn't know why you're waiting at the shakers." They looked at each other, and the younger one pointed to the older one, who had at least ten years of age on him, and gave him a nudge toward me. That was rig seniority, for you. It didn't matter if you were 50 or 15, only your rig years counted. They knew there needed to be someone watching the shakers but apparently forgot the whole part of someone needing to help weight up the system.

I made my way back to the floor and glanced at Vann as he stared at the gauges.

"Still the same," he said, reading my mind and knowing what I was looking for.

"Well, let's go ahead and screw into it that TIW and start pumping that eleven point six pound downhole."

"Gotcha." I grabbed my cup of coffee and took a sip, feeling the distasteful lukewarm taste follow. Couldn't even get a good cup of coffee. It was just one of those days. I seemed to think better when I had something to ease the habit in my blood, and coffee was a suitable substitute when whiskey was prohibited. Vann got things lined out with the derrick hand for pumping that 11.6-pound mud downhole, and I thought of the worm I had just sentenced to the painstaking task of throwing 100-pound sacks for the rest of his night. He probably didn't think of himself as the worm; most new guys won't accept the title, but the nudge from the other said different. Really, it was no big deal to be the worm; at least you only had to throw sacks, trip pipe and scrub. You wouldn't have to answer for this well if we lost control of it. Part of me wished I were back as a worm. I remembered a time when life was a lot less stressful. I knew of tool hands who hadn't had a good night's sleep in years, and multiple strokes from the mental agony and stress. Most turned into full-blown alcoholics due to the stress that was hidden deep in their bones. I constantly wondered if that would be my eventual outcome.

I looked out over the floor to the side of our rig site at the flare box burning a 45-foot flare from gas downhole that had traveled through our lines to the box. It was large enough to reflect the heat back to me even while I was standing over 75 yards away. It felt nice to have the flare warming up location in mid-October in North Dakota. I could tell this winter was going to be a doozy; they were already forecasting sub-zero temps by the end of the week.

Vann walked over and looked at the gauges as I took another sip of my lukewarm sludge. "Seven hundred and three hundred!" Vann shouted out to me.

"What? It's only been fifteen minutes!" I couldn't believe it. There was absolutely no way pressure should have dropped that quick.

"Yep. I don't know how, but that's where it's at."

"How many barrels of that eleven point six pound did you get downhole?"

"Sixty-five."

"That's not near enough, not even fucking close."

"Not supposed to be, but I guess it did the trick. You want me to stop pumping?"

"No. Get all that mud downhole, and we can go from there."

"Gotcha."

Vann picked up the phone with a rag in a futile effort

to stay semi-clean. I could tell that he had already wiped it down, but the sliminess of oil remained. "Derrick hand?"

"Yeah, Drill?"

"Go ahead and stop mixing that bar. We got things under control and are good to go." With that, he hung up. I was confused. It didn't make sense that he would shut that down.

"Vann, let's go ahead and keep that mixing and get some heavier mud ready." I wished we had talked about it before he made the call, but confusion was sometimes the name of the game.

"Derrick hand?"

"Yeah, Drill?"

"Keep mixing and get your pill tank filled with 13.5."

"Will do."

He looked back at me with a slight look of disgust. "You really want those guys to mix all that for nothing?"

"You're damn right I do. There is no reason our pressure should have declined like that. I want that fluid in the pits for backup."

"I suppose, but you probably just made us waste a bunch of bar and time."

"So be it." It was irrelevant to me if it wasted their time or their barite. I was only focused on one thing. I had no time to be concerned about a possible wasted effort. "There really was no reason that pressure should have declined." I thought about it more and more and couldn't come to a logical conclusion. I knew there were a bunch of oilfield mysteries that nobody would ever have an answer for, but for every mystery downhole, there is a legitimate problem solved, and the fact was that nobody was going to die on my shift if I had anything to say about it, and having 13.5-pound fluid on hand could save our rear ends in a pinch. Still, the fact remained that this made no sense, not one lick of it, and I was becoming quite uncertain that this was all over. Why in the world would pressure disappear suddenly? There was no explanation for it, at least not in this world, but the fact was that we weren't dealing with this world; we were dealing with the underworld.

CHAPTER 8

Midnight: 500 ft. Away from the Liner Top, 800 ft. Away from Desired Plug Setting Depth

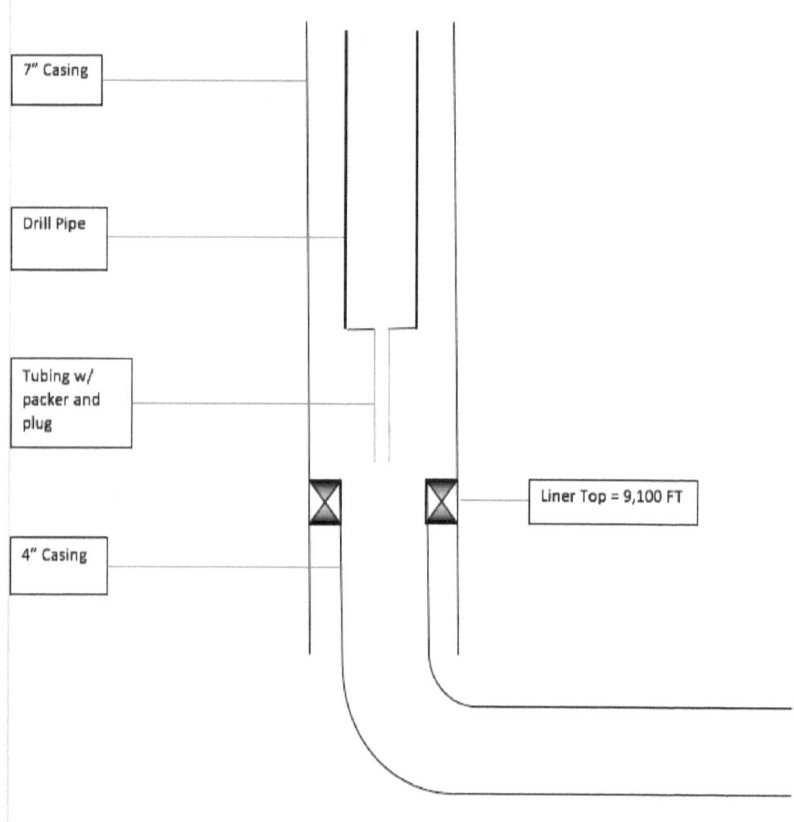

With the pressure gone, things were settling out now that there was 11.6-weighted mud in the hole. We continued the trip back downhole, screwing one stand of drill pipe into the other and lowering our tools deeper. The well was under control with nothing left to secure; we were now in control, with no pressure coming back to us. It still didn't make sense, but there was nothing we could do about it; if the pressure wasn't there, it wasn't there, and we had to continue. With close to 500 feet left until we encountered the Liner Top, we ran the next four stands. Even with each one close to 100 feet in length, we ran them in very easy.

I stood next to Vann as the brake handle leveled above his waist with his palm keeping it in check, allowing the rig to let the drill pipe to creep down. "Come on up, Vann, and let's get an up weight." I listened to the motors roar as he brought the drill string up, as they bellowed exhaust onto the floor. I noted that we were 120K with the drill string coming up, which was spot on with 11.6-pound mud in the hole. You could expect a significant weight change as the drill string is pulled up, allowing the string not to rest on anything in the hole and taking out any slack that the hole is taking. "Hold it steady." He stopped the drill string, and the whole rig sat silent. The indicator read *115K*, a clear neutral reading. "Okay, keep on going down." I noted that the weight dropped significantly, reading at *90K*, which was quite unusual; it indicated our hole was quite crooked, especially for being in the vertical section of a wellbore. We were prepared to try and get through Liner Top.

Vann glanced over at me. "You want Rikki up here?"

"Not really."

"You sure? I could call and tell him to get on up."

"Let him sit." As soon as I said it, we heard the steel door leading up to the floor slam shut. We turned around and got a full view of Mr. Tubs in blue coveralls. Rikki was back.

"You fuckers weren't even going to call me up for the set?"

I glanced at Vann with a slight smile. I always operated

under the impression that it wasn't my job to hold a consultant's hand, and it wasn't his job to hold mine. Maybe we should have called him. I apologized. "Sorry, Rikki, I didn't know if you wanted to be up here or not." The fact was that a lot of consultants couldn't have cared less—that's why they hired me.

His face wore an offended look, but my guess was that it wasn't the first time his feelings had been injured. "I need to be here any time you are setting tools. You got it?" He looked straight at me with a look that could kill.

"Feel free to join anytime." If he wanted to do his job, he could do it; if not, I wasn't going to go out of my way to inform him of every little thing. I could tell this guy wasn't really fond of me, but what did he want me to say? Oh, sir, master, highness, king, company man, let me be your servant, and whenever it's time for you to supervise and actually do your job, I will make sure and let you know, your majesty. On second thought, telling him to join us wasn't near as bad as what I wanted to tell him. It probably wasn't the best attitude to have, but nevertheless, it was the one I had developed.

Vann switched back gears, lowering the drill string, and I trained my eye on the weight indicator, desperately wishing to see a bobble indicating we went through that notorious Liner Top nice and smooth. The numbers showed we were just five feet away. We slowed the pipe to a crawl while we started taking weight that just wouldn't come back to us. I set 7,000 pounds down, hoping it would sink through, but no luck; my tools were hitting on the Liner Top. I stood over Vann with an eagle eye on the indicator, thinking of my decisions very carefully. It had to be the retrieving head on top of the plug getting us hung up because it had a mill tooth bottom. That fact created a twofold problem: if we turned to the right, we could possibly set our plug; if we turned to the left, we could possibly set our packer on top of the Liner Top and get it stuck. I weighed the options. The plug took close to four revolutions to the right to set, and the packer only took 3/4 of a revolution to the left to set, along with my retrieving head only taking a 1/4 turn to the left to release. Running in tandem was always a joy.

"Can you set that torque when you go to the left with this top drive?" I asked.

"Yep. Sure thing." I was glad to hear it; it was going to make the day just a little bit easier.

"Set slips and screw your top drive into that joint, and set your torque for no more than two thousand foot-pounds." Vann did it without questioning me. He was experienced enough to know the situation could become a complete nightmare if not approached carefully. I wasn't sure if he was aware of the common argument between tool hands about using a top drive for rotating packers downhole, just because of the torque you can get from a top drive, and most of them can't set their torque low enough or at all when turning to the left.

I opted to turn to the right due to the plug at the bottom took more revolutions to set. I had Vann set 2K down onto the Liner Top while turning a half turn to the right. Half a turn at 9100 feet downhole isn't much, but with the stiffness of drill pipe, it might give us what we needed.

Rikki stared at me, and my ears started feeling the screech of nails on a chalkboard as he spoke. "You sure you wanna do that?" He stood with his chubby arms crossed over his heavy chest.

I raised my eyebrows. "Pretty sure." Vann rotated the drill string ever so slightly to the right, half a turn.

No luck, though. I watched the needle on the indicator stay in place. I wanted it to come back to neutral at 115K. I was hoping 2,000 pounds resting on it with slight rotation would give it the convincing it needed, but it didn't; 2,000 pounds downhole was nothing due to deviations and the pipe hitting every wall of casing on the way down—what we like to call buckling—but buckling was pretty irrelevant with drill pipe, especially in a vertical hole. I reminded myself to not get carried away. There have been many tool hands who ripped their tools in half or set down too much weight and destroyed their tools because they got antsy. We were nowhere near that point yet. We could still set 50,000 pounds down if that's what I thought would get her through the Liner Top, but it wasn't.

I felt the insult of Rikki's words when he spoke. "Don't you want to go to the left?"

Sometimes I wondered how someone like him got this far in the oilfield. "Nope. Not really, Rikki."

"Well you should. Your tool inside the Liner sets to the right, and you're liable to get us planted and cock-locked right here."

I was appalled at his opinion and his lack of expertise and turned to express my frustration "I'm not fucking going to!" It was a bold stance to take, but to get a tiger off my back, it was worth it. I knew I wasn't going to set my tool, it was my tool, and it would take four revolutions to set it. I really needed him to just go back to his shack and shut up, but there was no way I would get that lucky.

I told Vann, "Set 4 K down on it, and put another half

turn to the right into her." He did, without question. I wanted just a bit of movement in order to drop the tools through the smaller diameter of our Liner Top. He paid no attention to Rikki, which I appreciated. I was starting to like this guy. I watched as the weight indicator edged back to 115K, setting us at neutral and relieving my nerves, which hopefully never showed as we glided our tools smoothly through the Liner Top. I had bad memories from a job a couple of years ago where we had been trying to slide tools through the Liner Top. After several days of trying, we ended up ripping the Liner Top out and being out there for close to a month. I was never so thankful to get a good night's rest as I was after I finished with that mess.

"Vann, ease her on down another three stands." That would give us close to the 300 ft. below the Liner Top that we needed to set our plug. About a hundred feet below that was a fracking sleeve that I was trying my damnedest to stay away from. If you ran into a fracking sleeve, it could bust wide open and their whole 2 million dollar fracking job would be completely wasted, and I would be sitting at the house biting my fingernails, hoping nobody put two and two together. It wasn't something I wanted to have to answer for.

We put the third stand all the way down to the floor.

I said, "Screw into her again so we can rotate." Vann complied as I watched the floor hands set slips so the pipe could rest in the hole while he lowered the big yellow school bus also known as a top drive screw into the box end of the drill pipe, which allowed us the ability to rotate.

"Raise up the string and have a hand measure eight feet from the floor so we got room to set."

Rikki glanced at me with questioning eyes. "You sure

eight feet will be enough?"

"Pretty sure, Rikki. I've set one or two of these before." I watched the top drive raise the pipe up as one of the floor hands measured the first 5 feet by making a thick yellow mark from a crayon he held before raising the pipe the other 3 feet.

"Put three more rounds to the right, and let's start slacking off slowly." Vann did so, and as we counted rounds, he crept down on the drill pipe. There was no indication of the plug starting to set, which was not what we wanted. We were at our down weight of 90K and had gone 3 feet past where we wanted a set.

I heard Rikki's annoying voice in my ear. "I'm telling you we need to start higher."

I paid no attention to him and stood there with Vann and instructed, "Come on back up to our eight foot mark and put two more wraps in it; just ease her down exactly how you did while rotating." We lowered the pipe to our 5 ft. mark, and I noticed the indicator start to bobble and take weight as I watched it read *85K, 80K, 75K, 70K*. Perfect. Just what we wanted. The plug was set. All that was needed was to pack off the elements and get the retrieving head off it, so we could move the packer up hole.

"All right, Vann, hold it there. Let's make sure those upper slips are setting for us. Pull twenty K over." I watched the moment of truth take place, waiting for the steel and carbide to bite the inner walls of the casing and pull over until I said stop.

I watched as Vann crept the pipe back up to 119K, bringing it past our 5-foot mark and I saw the infamous bobble on the indicator as the needle started walking upwards— *125k,130k,135k,140k.*

"All right, looks good. Go ahead and pack it off two more times just like that, going thirty K down on it and pulling over thirty K."

"You sure you wanna go that high, thirty K over?" Rikki asked over my shoulder.

"Pretty sure, Rikki." I sincerely tried not to say it rudely, but how do you treat stupidity when it goes on over and over? Vann kept looking at me as if he was a frayed rope in a tug of war game. "Go, ahead Vann, pack it off with thirty K."

Vann quickly nodded. "All right, boss." I always hated when a driller called me boss. He knew and I knew I wasn't. There was nothing I could order him to do; I was a guest on his rig, toolhand or not. I was simply here to help him get his well back in order, but one usually only called me boss if things were going right, so it was a compliment, nevertheless.

I watched as he packed the plug's elements off, sealing them against the inner walls of the casing, lowering drill pipe and letting 30,000 pounds of force set on my tool, then pulling 30,000 pounds over, stretching every piece of steel and rubber on the plug.

"All right, it's packed off. Come back to neutral weight."

"You sure?" Rikki asked. He sounded like a one-phrase parrot.

"Pretty sure, Rikki." I replied as I watched the indicator flick right at 115k. "Neutral. That's what we like to see. Now come down to ninety K and set ten more down on it, giving us eighty on the indicator. That will be just ten K down on the tool, and then we will work on releasing that retrieving head from the plug and coming up to set the packer."

"All right, boss." I didn't think I would be able to break him of his "boss" habit. It was definitely nothing for me to get upset about, but I still didn't like it, especially because he was older than me. Whether or not he knew it was a different story.

With the weight indicator setting at 80K and Vann still leaning on the brake handle, he turned around and looked at me, waiting for direction on what to do next. I stressed to him, "This is the vital part for us. I want you to put a half turn to the left in order to get the retrieving head to J off the plug."

"Got it, boss." It would almost be rude to correct him now, but it irked me every time, although not nearly as much as the sound of Rikki's voice articulating another query.

"You sure you know what you doing?" Rikki asked.

Now I sounded like the parrot. "Pretty sure, Rikki."

"How many times have you actually set these tools?"

I looked over and gave him a disbelieving death glare, especially since things were actually going fairly well, and hoped my reply would bolster his confidence. "This time plus one more will make two." Truth was I had thousands of sets under my belt, but it was no use trying to convince him of that. He just glared back at me without saying anything else.

Vann put in the half-round of left, keeping an eagle eye on his torque to make sure it didn't go over 2,000 pounds.

"Come on up slowly." I watched as Vann put the rig in gear and lifted up on the brake handle, raising the drill pipe slowly. I wouldn't know if we had gotten off the plug until the pipe got past the 8-foot mark and the needle was reading the customary up weight of 119-120K while raising the pipe.

"I think we're good," Vann said as the pipe sat 15 feet up.

I heard Rikki's voice crack over my shoulder. "You had better hope so." I turned and gave my best *what the hell* look and glared through his soul.

I turned back to Vann to give instruction. "Indeed. Go ahead and set that packer. Put another half turn to the left, which will give us a full wrap to the left with the previous half."

"Gotcha." He put the half-wrap in as I watched and eased up on the brake lowering the drill pipe as the indicator dropped down to 85K. The packer's slips started to bite against the inner walls as the plug had done and sealed off its own rubber elements.

"How much weight you want down on it?" Vann asked.

"Let's give her 20,000 pounds down."

"Will do." It was always a relief to have a good set and definitely refreshing to have two good sets. Vann looked over at me. "What's next?"

"Let's test down the drill pipe against the plug, which in turn will test that seven feet in between the packer and plug also. But we mainly just care if that plug is holding; it would be a pretty slim chance that those seven feet in that particular spot are our problem."

I watched as Vann grabbed the receiver and I heard the intercom spark up. "Derrick hand!"

"Yeah, Drill?"

"Line those pumps up so we can pump through the drill pipe and test this plug and packer."

"Yes, sir."

Vann tapped on his computer screen, brought up the

rig pump controls, and figured his parameters on the volume to pump.

It wasn't long before the derrick hand came back on the phone. "Lined out." Vann glanced over at me, awaiting approval to do what he already knew needed to be done.

"Go ahead."

"What pressure you want to see?"

"Give us four thousand psi down the drill pipe."

"Will do, boss." I watched as his gauges on the screen started climbing up with every ounce of fluid being pumped down to my plug.

"One thousand psi!" Vann called out as the needle poked its head to the one representing a thousand.

"Keep coming up with it."

"Two thousand psi."

I glanced over at Vann with a slight bit of concern. "Have a guy go check the backside and make sure it's not leaking." Things looked good on the gauge, but a visual check was always a good reassurance.

"Will do, boss," he said and immediately called Dakotah to tell him to do so.

"Three thousand psi!" Vann shouted to me.

"Right on. Keep her moving," I said.

"Four thousand psi." Vann tapped the button on the screen to shut it down.

"Right on the money. Let's see if she will hold for us." We watched the gauge like a hawk watching mice in a field as the needle steadily dropped lower until it settled at 3600 psi.

"Is that going to be all right?"

"Not really."

"What you wanna do about it?"

"Let's just give it a minute or two and see if it goes any lower." Once you start pressuring pipe, strange things can occur. Patience was key; we waited to see if it would leak off any more.

"All right, boss." I made my way to the dog house to refill my cup of joe, liquid fuel that was as dark as the oil in south Texas. My nostrils filled with the steam and aroma of the brew as I poured my Styrofoam full.

"What are you reading now, Vann?"

"Thirty-two hundred psi."

"Damn it." I wished I could go downhole and view my tools for myself to see if they were possibly leaking, but I was taught by old timers that you had to have faith in what you set. It didn't help that I could feel Rikki's stare along with his nagging.

"You probably set too much weight on that packer," Rikki said as I walked in front of him while sipping my cup of joe.

I turned around to meet him eye to eye with a smile, something he didn't return. "You think so?"

"Yeah, I do. Question is, what the hell you gonna do about it?"

I just smiled. It always amused me that when anything remotely went wrong, the consultant had to play the blame game. I would have hated to be in a sandbox as a kid with most company men; they couldn't build their own castle, but they could sure tell you what you did wrong on yours.

I was halfway tempted to set another 20,000 lbs. down on it just to prove a point, but it wasn't worth it in case something did happen.

"Vann, bring that pressure back up to four thousand

psi," I said.

"Will do, boss."

I watched the needle climb back up to 4,000 as Rikki's arms crossed in an accusatory pose. "We can't just sit here all night watching a fucking gauge!"

I watched as the needle dropped to 3,800 then to 3,600. "Vann call up and make sure nothing is coming out the backside." Vann picked up the phone to check with Dakotah, who was watching the very thing that would tell us if the packer was allowing fluid to come up around us. I waited anxiously for the reply.

"Nope, nothing coming out," I heard come through the receiver.

With that, knowing I had every right, I turned directly to Rikki. "You need to go check all your fucking iron." It was all I could think to say, and it really wasn't his iron, it was Vann's, but it didn't matter. If Big Rikki was going to pester me and wanted to be a part of things, well, then, he got his wish. There was nothing else that needed to be said. He knew that he had overstepped his boundaries and that I had had enough of his nonsense. It always seems that company men feel like they are helping when they crawl up your ass. Do they really think it helps? It only itches.

Rikki slammed the steel door leading down the stairs as he disappeared, madder than a hornet hopped up on red pepper, but I liked it. Vann and I just smiled at each other and shook our heads.

"He's something else."

"Yeah, and it ain't just you. You should see him when things really hit the fan. He doesn't know his ass from a hole in the ground."

"I believe it." I pondered what Rikki would do if it ever hit the fan. "Well, Vann, we really do need to check those pump lines and valves to make sure it's not leaking on surface."

"You really think it's going to be leaking up here?"

"I sure hope so, after talking to Rikki like that." I cracked a smile as I recalled how pissed off Rikki was.

Vann's cheeks creased in a smile that flashed back toward me. "I bet. I would be hoping so too. Hell, if you don't get run off by the end of this job, hats off to you." The thoughts started creeping up on me of possibly getting run off on my first job back, and I wondered what Bryant would think about it. Vann interrupted my thoughts. "I will have that derrick hand get on it and see if he can find a leaky valve or something that got left open."

A lot of times you don't have to be so precise on pressure, but this time was different. We had to be on the money with this. I didn't want to see our gauges bleed off even 50 psi, much less 400 psi.

I waited and sipped my liquid fuel, feeling the caffeine energize my system. They say that coffee is America's worst drug problem, but I've never felt that way, although that's probably what any addict would say. I took another sip. There was something about having a fresh cup in your hand; it may have been an addiction, but I just liked the way the cup filled my hand. Somebody once told me that coffee releases endorphins in your brain. I wasn't sure what that entailed exactly, but it must have had something to do with calming the nerves. I sat on the steel bench resting in the driller's cabin that we called the doghouse and waited for the test results from the trusty derrick hand like a sick patient waiting for a diagnosis.

CHAPTER 9

"Found it!" I heard our trusty derrick hand yell over the rig phone; Vann picked it up immediately and held it out so I could hear.

"Where's it at?" I asked.

"On the pump line. There's a union that's spewing out."

"How bad?" I asked.

"Bad enough."

"Can you fix it?" Vann asked

"Does a bear shit in the woods and wipe his ass with a white rabbit?"

"You just get it fixed or you're going to be the white rabbit."

"It may take a couple minutes, but I'll get her."

"Let me know if you want daddy to come down there." Vann looked over at me with a smirk as we waited for a response.

Over the receiver came the derrick hand's reply. "Come on, Big Daddy!" Vann glanced back at me, oil still dripping out of his beard, knowing he had just pushed the right buttons to get a rise.

"I was afraid you would say that," Vann yelled back with a chuckle. "Just get it fixed! If I got to do it, then I don't need you!" That was true, and I think the derrick hand realized it too. There was a quick acquiescence.

"All right, boss. I'll have it fixed up pretty quick."

Vann hung up the receiver and he looked over at me.

"Wyatt, you're a lucky dog, I tell you."

"How you figure?"

"Cause ol' Rikki down there was probably making a phone call to run your ass off if they hadn't of found a leak."

"Don't threaten me with a good time, cold beer and warm women; I'll be at the house in no time." We laughed, knowing very well that Rikki probably would like to see me dismissed and it was becoming less and less important to me. At least this leak might add a little credibility to my name. It's pretty hard to run a guy off if he's right, although it has been done.

We staggered into the driller's cabin with the snow still floating down and the flakes thickening, making their way onto the back of my neck. I sat my hardhat down beside me on the bench, and I leaned back against the lockers. The metal was comfier than I thought. I would have settled for just about anything at that point due to the lack of sleep from the night before. Even a bed of stone would provide my mind rest. It was pushing close to two a.m., and I felt like the most worthless being in the world for wanting to nap, but I could feel the effects from the lack of sleep; my mind slowly began to fade out, as if it had been injected with a dose of heavy syrup.

. . . .

"It's fixed, Drill!" I didn't want to open my eyes. Vann nudged my boots. It must have been the derrick hand over the intercom. I glanced at my watch through the scratches on my safety glasses and realized I had been dozing for fifteen minutes. I knew I had gone soft. One night without sleep, and I dozed off on the lockers; it used to be that if I got one hour every three days, I was good to go. I gathered my bearings and slapped my hardhat onto my skull as I planted my feet underneath me.

"Are you sure it's fixed?" I heard Vann ask.

Vann held the receiver out for me to hear the derrick hand's reply. "Yeah, it's fixed. No need to bring yourself down here, brother bear." Vann chuckled to himself.

"All right. Good job, white rabbit." Vann looked over at me, curiosity written on his face. "What you wanna do, boss?"

"Bring the pressure on up to four thousand and let's see if we can get a test." I made my way back over to the coffee pot that had fueled me. Thankfully, there were still some dregs left. I poured some into my oil-stained Styrofoam cup and reached into the mini-fridge for some creamer. I tossed a shot in, took off my safety glasses, and stirred with one of the arms. Trick of the trade.

"You get there yet?" I yelled over to Vann as he brought up the pressure.

"Three thousand and counting." I walked back over to him and glanced at the gauge. We watched the needle rise to 4000 psi as Vann shut the pumps down.

I looked at Vann as he looked at me. "Now that's what we want to see," he said.

I sipped my coffee and replied, "Yeah, buddy, hold it there for about five minutes and let's get a test."

"Will do." I watched as the needle held steady. There was no movement, not one bit. Perfect. We waited and bled the pressure off. I spotted the needle of the drill pipe gauge starting to increase instead of decreasing.

Vann looked at me "4500 psi." I nodded with a slight confusion on the pressure increase and kept watching.

"Double check your pumps."

"They are off."

"I don't give a shit, double check!" I snapped back as I watched Vann walked back to check his screens and gauges. "6000 psi!" I yelled to Vann.

"They are fucking off!"

"7000!" I screamed.

"What do you want to do!" My mind stalled as I debated our very few options in split seconds.

"Let's get that IBOP shut before that kelly hose bust!"

BAM! It sounded as if a gun had gone off, and I felt a rush of fluid sending me barreling into Vann, knocking him over as we crashed behind the driller's stand. Invert and oil spewed out of the floor uncontrollably as gas continued to blow from the oversized hose. Flat on my back, I looked up as the hose whipped from the derrick leg to derrick leg uncontrollably from the pressure like a massive black anaconda looking for its next victim. I quickly glanced back over to where Vann had been. The pressure had pushed him across the floor. His face had landed on the business end of a pipe-wrench jaw; a mass of blood was erupting from his forehead and covered his cranium. He laid there not moving.

Invert and oil poured over our bodies as I circled around the draw works to bypass the whipping hose and the deadly high pressure fluid. I shook his body violently. I felt a sharp pain in my shoulder, as if it had been hit with a brick, but that was the least of my worries. "Vann! Get Up!" There was no response, no movement, no blink of an eye. I grabbed his jaw tightly and shook him wildly. Blood spilled from his mouth as he regained consciousness. I felt horrible that it was me who delayed a decision. I wish I had been given more time to think but oilmen were not always given such luxury.

He looked at me as he came to with blood still draining from a deep gash above his left eye and a busted lip producing even more blood that dripped down his shirt. He blurted out, "We got to shut that IBOP!" He staggered over to his screen that controlled the IBOP valve that would close off pressure from below.

I watched as the screen flashed indication of the valve being pushed closed by the power of hydraulics as the pressure ceased, verifying that Vann had successfully closed it off. I ran down to the accumulator and closed the rams that secured the outside of the pipe.

Vann bent over and picked a tooth up off the floor that had been lying next to the jaw of the 36" pipe wrench. "You all right, man?"

I watched as he looked at his tooth in his palm and back at me. "Yeah, I'll make it. How about yourself?"

He wiped the blood from his head and tried to wipe the oil from his arms, putting the tooth in his pocket. "I'm good," I told him. I looked over at the eye wash station that was covered in fluid. Oil dripped from my soaked skull, and I took a clean rag to my eyes and face.

"What the hell happened there?" Vann asked.

I surveyed the floor and pointed up. "Kelly hose busted." The massive hose could not hold the pressure that had come back to us from the underworld and had busted. There was no way to know the true pressure of what we had just encountered. Everything had just happened so fast.

I felt a nagging pain streak through my shoulder but knew it to be minor compared to Vann's injuries. I sat him inside his steel cabin and started bandaging him up as best I could, using anything I could grasp from the first aid kit that hung on the wall in the driller's cabin.

Vann shook his head in disbelief as he stared outside at the oil-covered floor. "I can't believe that just happened."

"Me neither. Something very strange is going on here."

"You're telling me." I looked at him, he looked at me, and we shook our heads at one another, both covered in sludge, looking like well spent oilmen faded in a black and white photograph from years ago.

Vann grabbed the receiver. "Derrick hand, pick up."

"Yeah, Drill?"

"Get us lined up on that gas buster, so we can start burning off some of this gas."

"Will do. Anything else?"

Vann looked over at me, and I nodded in agreement to the only thing that Vann could possibly want to know. "Yeah, get us weighted up."

"Will do." With that, he hung up the receiver.

....

Invert and oil covered the derrick legs, turning the white iron legs a deep, dark brown. The oil dripped down and added to the puddles on the floor. There was no clean spot on the floor; everything was covered in ooze, and the stench of diesel and chemicals that people usually wear hazmat suits for filled the air. I shook my head and looked up at the crown of the rig and gave thanks to the Man upstairs for letting me make it through the ordeal. I shook my head and chalked up one more close call. These episodes were the battle stories in our line of work. Some guys relished them and talked about them any chance they could. Personally, I always felt like I could prevent anything bad from happening if I just did my job right. It should never happen. NEVER! There were no excuses for it, but in all my training and all of my experience, I couldn't sort it out. It didn't make sense. Why is this pressure going away but coming back with such a fury?

We heard the steel door slam open. The noise was as dreadful as the clang of a prison cell door slamming shut. After a moment, Rikki wiggled through the door, plump and still wearing oversized faded blue coveralls—stain-free. At least he was clean. "What the hell did you boys do?"

Vann and I looked at each other, trying to figure out if he was pissed or just joshing. I couldn't tell, so I erred on the side of caution and started explaining what had happened event by event at least what I knew, since he genuinely seemed to care for this one brief moment.

"Anybody hurt?"

I figured I'd let Vann answer however he saw fit. When I looked down waiting for Vann's reply, I noticed Rikki's feet were covered by tan leather house shoes. It was no time to laugh, but I had to chuckle inside. Vann remained quiet; he was missing a tooth and had blood dripping through the Band-Aids on his forehead I had put on, and he didn't know what to say.

I heard a dreadful sigh from Vann, and he finally muttered, "No, sir." I figured that's what he'd say. Getting injured on a rig was a funny thing; you never admitted it unless you had to because of the pile of paperwork you had to deal with and the fact that you were labeled a safety hazard and to top it all off, lose your safety bonus. One way or another, it was your fault if you got hurt.

"You good then, Vann?" asked Rikki.

He raised his head and looked Rikki in the eye, missing tooth and blood dripping from his forehead, he said, "Yes, sir." He breathed heavily as he let it out, knowing it was an OSHA-recordable incident, and he might have to foot the bill for those two simple words. I'm sure Rikki felt the relief of not having to make the phone call saying he got a guy injured on his watch. It was a phone call no one wanted to make. Hiding injuries wasn't always a good idea, but sometimes the repercussions from the injury were worse than the injury itself. I couldn't blame Vann; he didn't want to deal with the bullshit.

Rikki turned and paced for a moment before revealing what was on his mind. "We need to weight up again."

Vann wiped the blood from his forehead and replied, "Yes, sir, my derrick hand is already working on it." Rikki nodded in response.

I interjected, pointing up at the big black hose busted and hanging against the derrick. "We won't be pumping anything before that gets fixed," I said.

Rikki's face filled with disgust. "Damn it! What should we do then, Wyatt?"

"There is nothing we can do until this rig gets fixed." We all grew quiet as the realization hit us: we were sitting ducks.

"We need to unset and weight up, but in order to do that, we have to get that Kelly hose fixed."

Rikki spoke up. "I want to see if we can get that packer unset and let things equalize."

I crossed my arms and sighed deeply at the stupidity but tried to remain respectful. "Not a good idea."

"Why not?" Rikki asked.

"It's just not. Think about it."

"I have fucking thought about it."

I tried to contain my frustration. "It's better to leave it shut in and fix things; it won't make a difference if that packer gets unset or if it even moves."

"Well, I want to see it move, and I would like the well equalized," Rikki replied.

"Okay, then that's what we shall do." I looked over at Vann. "All right, get your bag shut and your rams open so we can move."

"Yes, sir."

I watched as Vann pushed buttons and called in for verification. Rikki and I waited in silence until I looked over at him and spoke. "This is stupid."

He glared over at me and replied, "If you don't like it, you are sure welcome to leave."

"Don't threaten me with a good time." I turned back around, waiting for him to follow through with his threat of running me off, but it never came.

Vann turned to both of us. "If you women are done bickering, we are ready to move pipe."

I stepped up beside Vann and instructed, "Let's pick up nice and easy to our neutral weight." Vann nodded in response as I continued instruction. "It's only a straight pick up to release the tool. We should see the unloader open first on the weight indicator, and once that happens, we will shut down and let that pressure settle out between the casing and pipe."

"Sounds good." As he started picking up the drill pipe, I didn't see any change on the gauges. I watched as the pipe crept up in case the pressure was making things act funny. I watched as the indicator got to 150,000, meaning 30,000 pounds of tension pulled into my packer.

"Let's hold it there and come on back down, something's not right." It didn't seem as if anything was moving. I literally needed to just pick straight up. That was the beauty of the HD packer—straight pick up to release—but it wasn't happening, not one bit. It wasn't budging, so it seemed.

"Come on back down; we might have something on top of us." Vann did as asked, and I took note of Rikki coming up behind me to watch what was going on.

"Having issues?"

"Yeah, just not acting right." My statement didn't provide much hope, but it was true. "All right, Vann, let's try it again. Come on back up till you get to one-fifty K." I felt my nerves start to tense as the needle climbed up to 145K, with no give at 150K. "All right, Vann. Come on down fast and hit that bitch like it's your ex-wife."

Vann's head kicked back in laughter with blood starting to dry on the side of his head. "I only wish." He clutched out, letting the blocks fall, burying drill pipe through the floor and pushing weight down to my packer. The needle sunk lower as he slammed weight downhole. The vibrations pulsated up the steel floor and through my boots, making every nerve in my body tense. I had little expectation that it would work and set it free.

"Vann, do what you want with it, just don't pull 175 K. I got to talk with Rikki." I motioned for Rikki and me to talk in the doghouse.

As we entered, Rikki voiced what was on both of our minds. "You going to be able to get this shit out of the hole?"

"No, probably not. At least not yet. We need to shut down and get this rig fixed." I would have loved to say yes, but I just didn't see it happening, I thought seriously about lying and elevating his hopes, but I didn't feel like playing the game. Playtime was over, we were done, stuck like chuck. At least that was my thought; then my ears registered a sudden POP! come from the drill pipe as it jumped, and Vann looked over at me with a smile, showing off the gap where a tooth only recently took up space.

"Got it!" I still wasn't sure, but it was promising. The string started moving freely, and a smile streaked across Vann's face, cracking the dried blood on his cheek.

"You sure you didn't just part your fucking tool?" Rikki asked.

"Pretty sure, Rikki." It was a fact that my tool was the weakest link in the string, but we were well below specs for parting. I managed to keep smiling. I still had to listen to this moron's thoughts, he was the boss, even though I would have loved to stick him down a sewer drain and let him rot.

"I fucking hope so." I turned back to see that Vann had stopped smiling, and the needle was climbing steadily upwards to 150k as Vann slowed the drill pipe to a halt. Rikki shook his head in frustration and walked off the floor at a loss of what to hope for. We were officially stuck again.

"Regardless, something changed," I said.

I watched as Rikki made his chubby way behind me from the doghouse with an apology in his voice. "Good job, Wyatt. Come on down and talk with me when you get a chance." With that, he was gone again, down the stairs and slapping the steel door shut. It wasn't good to be stuck again, but it showed that my tool wasn't parted and something had changed in our favor.

"Maybe he ain't so bad," I said. Vann just laughed.

"He can be all right sometimes, although he definitely ain't no lucky charm."

"Hell, I don't think any of us are."

"Apparently not. We'll be lucky to make it out of this one alive if things keep going how they have been."

"I'm going to head on down and talk with Big Rikki. I'm not sure what he wants to do, but I would imagine he would want to assess the damages and get your rig fixed back up, then weight up."

"Yeah, we shall see. You never know with that guy," Vann mused. I filled my cup, wishing there was something stronger than coffee on location to fill my belly and my mind with. I was overdue for sleep whether they shut down or not. My mind was tired, but I knew there to be no rest for the wicked. Coffee would help me make it through the next hour or two. I made my way down to Big Rikki's shack, where he sat on the phone discussing the ordeal with engineers in Denver. I stripped my boots and kicked them to the side of Rikki's house shoes, which brought another chuckle out of me. I waited and hoped that the phone call would end shortly, but instead, Rikki put it on speakerphone and the questions poured in from the engineers. I explained everything I could, but they fired off endless questions that went nowhere. There was truly no cut and dried explanation for what was going on. We were getting pressure sometimes and not getting it others, we were stuck sometimes and able to move others, and we were able to circulate some times and not others. There was no explanation.

They finally hung up when they realized that it was impossible to reach any real conclusion. Rikki looked at my oil-soaked, disheveled clothes and the weary, glazed look in my eye and told me, "We're going to shut down and get the rig fixed. It might take a day or two, depending on how things go. Why don't you head on out and get a shower and some rest. I will call you when we're ready."

Those were the very best words I could have heard. It was as though he had just sent me to heaven. A shower and some rest would do me well. "Will do. I'll discuss options with Bryant and will give you a call when I get up, and we can talk about which way you want to go."

"Sounds good. Now go get some damn sleep, Wyatt. I'm going to need you on top of your game when you get back." I've always thought most company men were schizophrenic; one second they hate your guts and are crawling up your ass for every move you make, and the next they are your best friend. Trying to figure them out made me even more tired. I welcomed the opportunity for sleep.

"Will do."

CHAPTER 10
Meeting Zebb, June 2008

Sweat dripped down the back of my neck from the heat of a southeast Texas summer that would have had made an African monkey perspire. It continually drenched my oil-stained work shirt that hadn't been changed in days because we had been working around the clock to replace a Liner hanger that had preset on the trip in. The Liner hanger held the horizontal casing that sat deep in the well and suspended itself in the vertical section; getting it out was always very tricky, and even though I was back in my homeland, my blood was too thick from one too many years up North, and the heat drenched me day in and day out.

Still, I had entertainment nonetheless that I would never forget. I was working with a fishing hand that had about 35 years on me, Zebb Morgan, who grew on me over time. For over 45 days, we worked to repair the Liner hanger. We finally caught a break, completed the job, and had some time to kill before we flew out. I remember it well. We pulled into the local honkytonk joint with a flashing billboard advertising "Roughnecks Welcome: 1st Beer Free," but after about five or six Budweisers and a couple shots of Jack Daniel's to celebrate, I started to wonder if the sign might come down after they got done with us. We ran into issues when Zebb decided to tell a story about some crazy American working in Saudi Arabia.

I sat at the knotted pine bar, feeling the smoothness of the epoxy that had been coated many times over as Zebb slid my shot of Jack Daniel's down to me and started in on his story. He sat to my right, and a young roughneck sat on my left. Zebb rambled on as the young roughneck bent his ear and eavesdropped. "He was legendary, I tell you, legendary! There wasn't a tool he couldn't run, nor a well he couldn't fix. He was among the best and the baddest, and he would have eaten every one of your lunches."

Others were starting to listen since his voice was starting to carry farther across the bar. I had worked with this man for the last 45 days, and he was quite the jester, but good to work with; his knowledge exceeded that of any fishing hand I had met. However, therein lay the problem; most fishing hands believe they are the second coming, and they have no problem letting other people know it.

I glanced down the bar at a young roughneck who had been working with us for the last 45 days; he finally spoke up, slurring his words from the effect of the alcohol. "Whoo-o-o g-g-gives a sh-h-h-it? T-t-take your s-s-story and sho-o-ove it right up your ass. This is Texas, and if your s-s-story ain't about a T-T-Texas oil legend, shut the fuck up." I had heard his opinion before, only it had had a North Dakota ring to it. It seemed like the personnel in every oil field I went to thought the ones in other places were idiots. There was a part of me that sided with the rig hand; maybe it was the Texan part, who knew? North Dakotans were even thoughtful enough to come up with a bumper sticker for it all: "T.A.F.T.—This Ain't Fucking Texas." It was one of those real intelligent things you usually saw plastered on the same jacked-up trucks that would be repo's if the boom died. I guess you always had those guys.

Zebb was in fact a big man; he stood 6' 2" with a ponytail that draped clear down to the middle of his back and had big, calloused hands that could grab a young boy's head and squeeze the juices right out him. Even with an oversized beer belly that probably dated back to the late 70s, he still had the spunk of a wild man and was definitely somebody you wanted on your side if things broke out. I halfway expected Zebb to waylay the drunken loudmouth across the bar, but there was none of that. He sat calm and took his shot of Jack and chased it with a sip of Budweiser. "Let me tell you, sonny boy, this man would kick your ass up and down this bar if he found out you were doubting his stories. He got this reputation all from a well in Kuwait when the fires were going. He's probably half the reason you can still put gas in your tank. It was said that he could walk on location, and the fires would stop, and the wells would shut themselves down." He slammed his fist on the bar as he yelled toward the young roughneck. "THEMSELVES, I TELL YOU! DROPPED PIPE WOULD COME FLOATING BACK TO THE SURFACE FOR HIM IF HE SAID THE WORD! COME FLOATING BACK TO THE SURFACE!"

"B-b-bullshit," the roughneck retorted across to Zebb. I sat in the middle of this drama shaking my head in embarrassment but slightly and sadly enjoying the entertainment.

"I'm telling you, it was said that he dined with the sheiks and made friends with a many of the top officials. I even heard they would bring strippers out to location just to dance for him while he worked on wells. They would take him to the best clubs in Dubai, and a night out on the town was nothing unusual."

"Sh-u-u-ut da fuck u-u-up!" the roughneck muttered. Not the words I would have chosen, but I guess every man picks his own. I watched as Zebb ordered up a shot of Patron, licked salt from his hand, and pounded the shot of Tequila, slamming the glass on the table when he finished.

"I'm telling you, one night was different though—it was no regular gathering, it was only for the best. They hired dancers with bodies laced with the finest of jewels. They would dance all day and love all night, was the way the story goes." I chuckled to myself and took a swig from my bottle of Budweiser. Zebb told the story as if he was telling a kid a long-lost Halloween tale that was destined to change his life.

"Y-o-o-o-u are s-o-o-o full of sh-i-i-it, but come on let's hear it, big man. G-g-go ahead and fin-ishhh the t-t-tale."

I watched and listened; most of the bar was by now doing the same. Zebb took his last swig of Bud. "All right, I will tell you, but you got to shut your mouth."

I watched as the young roughneck leaned into the bar as he spoke. "A-l-l r-right, jus-s-s-st tell the fuck-ingg st-o-o-r-ry." His slur was definitely getting worse. He reached for another shot, and I realized he had probably lost count of how many he had had.

Zebb's face reddened, and his veins were starting to show, but he still seemed fairly calm somehow. I didn't expect this composure out of him. I thought he would have wiped the bar with this young roughneck by now. "All right, young'un, I'll tell it. You just have to shut the fuck up." He paused for a moment waiting for a response as the young roughneck motioned for him to continue. "You see, It was a cold night in the Saudi desert, and things went south at this particular gathering due to a slight disagreement between an official and the American. It was due to the American letting a pretty young thing keep dancing on him. This sheik insisted he get a different girl, and it started as a simple disagreement but eventually got intense and louder."

"K-k-kind of like you—LOUD?"

"Yeah, kind of like that. Just shut the fuck up and listen, young whipper-snapper, and you might learn something."

The young man, pretended to be scared. He waved his hands in the air like a ghost, dripping with sarcasm, howled, "OOOOOOOOH!" I just had to laugh. There was no doubt that somebody was going to pound this guy's face in by the time this was over. The young rig hand motioned for the story to continue and took the last gulp of his Bud. His speech was one long slur as the alcohol started to overwhelm him. "W-e-e-l-l? G-g-go a-h-head and t-el-l-l-l the fucking s-t-o-o-o-r-r-y."

"Well, as the story goes, the sheik got very, very angry 'cause of this little disagreement and the fact this cocky American would utterly disrespect a sheik in his own country. The sheik yelled out that SHE WAS HIS BLOOD! Apparently, this young lady was his long-lost niece and had somehow or another found her way into a glorified Saudi whorehouse. He ordered security to get this lowly piece of shit fishing hand

out of the club immediately and throw him to the birds. He got stripped naked and blindfolded, with his hands taped behind his back, and kicked out of the club.

"W-w-w-wait, Wait, Wait! N-n-naked! You are s-o-o-o-o f-f-f-u-u-u-ll of sh-i-i-it!"

I looked over and noticed Zebb's face start to tense and his veins about to pop in aggravation. There was only one thing that I could do for him. I stood up, got the barmaid's attention, and pointed at Zebb's empty bottle. "Another Budweiser for my fellow."

She nodded. "Sure thing."

Zebb started to continue his story. "Now you gotta listen, young'un." I couldn't help but wonder why in the world he wanted to tell this stupid story to this punk, but regardless, he was hellbent on telling it, and I figured it was useless to try and stop him. Buying his beer while he told it was a cheap price for the entertainment.

"You see, he made an easy target: white, American, and loud. They piled him into a Mercedes that smelled of dog dung and hauled him out of Dubai. While they drove, they constantly drove their fist into his gut, punching him like the dog they told him he was, and even stabbed him twice. But he counted every turn even as the knife entered his gut as they drove him out to the desert and dragged him out of the car by his longhaired ponytail. They left him there for dead. For over 12 days, he stumbled around in the desert over 100 miles from Dubai, but it's said that he was able to find water using the old witching method with a couple twigs he happened to land on when being thrown out. He found his way to the nearest oil rig by counting back the turns and got help from several roughnecks who found him stumbling around looking like death warmed over. They had some laughs, but they helped him anyways 'cause they knew who they had encountered."

"Th-th-that's the b-i-g-g-est line of b-b-bull-s-shit I have ever h-e-a-r-d! You p-p-probably seen that shit on B-la-ack Go-ol-ld last night!

You're a m-o-o-o-r-o-n!"

I shook my head at the young roughneck egging this giant of a man on, pushing every button he could, and I wished he would just buy into the bullshit and let it go, but he wouldn't. He looked over at his buddies, who had put down their pool cues and started watching the commotion. He tried again, like he was rallying support for his position like a politician on a campaign. "I'm calling b-u-l-l-s-s-shit, total b-u-l-l-s-shit! It's totally r-r-ridiculous! And you're a m-o-r-o-n!"

Zebb kept his cool, took a slug of beer, and glanced over to me. He gave me a nod of thanks for the beer and quietly spoke to the young rig hand. "Believe what you will, but I've lived it, sonny boy. That's my story." Zebb pulled up his shirt, revealing two eerie scarred wounds on the side of his overgrown body.

Quiet as a mouse, the drunken rig hand looked straight at Zebb with the most disgusted look and spouted slurs from his mouth. "That even con-f-i-r-r-m-s-s-s it, you're a big, fat, stupid ogre! You probably st-a-a-b-b-ed yourself j-j-u-u-u-st so you could tell this st-u-u-upid story. You couldn't find water in a fucking s-s-s-wim-ming p-p-pool, much less a desert in the Middle East."

That did it for old Zebb. It wasn't the loudness that infuriated him—he was probably used to that—it was the seriousness of calling him a liar along with calling him a big, fat, lying ogre. Zebb's face reddened in fury as he slammed his beer down on the bar, shattering the bottle into pieces that spattered across the bar and spilled onto the floor along with a liquid pool of beer. The distinct smell of Budweiser lingered as he rose with a wild look in his eyes. A fierce right hand dealt a devastating blow to the young roughneck's jaw. Clocked! I watched the young man's cheek turn and his body followed as his skull hit the wooden floor, and Zebb's broken bottle shards pierced his face. I spun on my stool and took a swig of my beer as Zebb jumped on the young man and took a fierce grab of the drunk's jugular. With Zebb's clinched fist raised past his own ear and the young man's eyes bulging with fear and pain as Zebb's grip tightened on his throat, I watched Zebb. He seemed to be deep in thought. For just about a second or two it seemed the whole bar was waiting on whether his fist would fall. I could only imagine what his struggle was. It looked to me like he had a battle going on within himself that was probably much fiercer than the one he was currently fighting on the outside. I waited and hoped for the fist to quietly unclench and fall—maybe Zebb regretted the first punch—but the only lowering was when the fist fiercely came down, connecting straight into the young roughneck's nose, splitting it wide open. Blood rushed out, spewing all over the wooden floor that his legs had recently rested on while insulting Zebb. Both of the young roughneck's hands tried furiously to get out of Zebb's gorilla grip on his throat as he exhausted every ounce of strength trying to squirm away, but there was no escaping. Zebb's unrelenting fist flew down again and again on the young man's bloody face. My heart quietly broke as I watched the young punk spew more and more blood, not for him who couldn't shut his mouth, but for Zebb.

There was a part of me that knew he was better than this, knew that he had given into something more than an insult, and now his anger fanned anew with every connected punch. I could have asked him to stop, if not for the man below Zebb, then for himself, but I knew there was no point. I watched as the young man's rig crew ran over, surely thinking enough was enough. They gave Zebb a chance to let up as they pleaded with him. They told him their friend was being idiotic, that he didn't know how to keep his mouth shut when he had been drinking, but the damage was done. There was no let-up in Zebb; if he was going to fight, he was going to fight the whole bar. I watched as one more blow buried deep into the young rig hand's face and blood spewed from the punk's nose. I finished the beer in front of me, not wanting any part of the mess. Maybe there was a sickness inside me that enjoyed the show, the feeling of revenge that was being served, but I also couldn't totally push back the things my eyes had seen when Zebb had the chance to lower his fist.

Finally, with their buddy bleeding and them unable to convince Zebb to stop, two of the crew members jumped on Zebb while their driller, weighing in at about 320, sat about four stools down from me watching the monkey show in earnest and cheering the whole mess on. One rig hand was on Zebb's back and had a stranglehold around his neck while trying to lock in a choke. I knew this wasn't going anywhere good when the second rig hand grabbed ahold of a metal chair that had sat quietly at their table and slammed it on old Zebb's skull. I saw the kid's face turn pale when Zebb just looked up at him as the kid held the chair dented by his skull. He looked as a child awaiting punishment from his father. I guess he didn't realize how hardheaded the old fishing hand was. One more joined in. Built like a German Panzer and I figured him to be their derrick hand; he punched Zebb square in the back of the head. Zebb's head came down as his eyes flowed back into his skull; his grip loosened on the kid's jugular as he toppled over on top of him, and he lay there, out cold. Zebb wasn't moving. He lay there helpless as the kid below him tried to seize the opportunity to escape from beneath the mammoth Zebb but wasn't able to due to the weight of Zebb and the lack of energy that had been sucked out of him from the beating he received.

The roughneck's crew continued their furious assault. The whole place seemed full of hate. I watched as the Panzer delivered a steel toe straight to Zebb's face as he lay there motionless, knocking two of his teeth across the floor. Zebb's eyes started to open at the shock of the kick; he looked over at me in desperation for some kind of help as the derrick hand climbed on his back and began to strike Zebb's skull with full-blown haymakers.

The gloves had come off and now anything went. I had no chance to consider the consequences of my actions. My blood boiled at the sight of Zebb's teeth skidding across the floor and the beating that continued. Any hope of avoiding this mess was long gone. If I walked out, they might kill him; if he happened to get the upper hand, he would probably kill them. I didn't make a habit of fighting. I had trained in mixed martial arts for a couple of years and had some dark alley fights under me from years ago. In a fight, I was the junkyard dog—the dog who went for the throat and ripped out your jugular, who would take your kneecaps out with a baseball bat and beat your skull in until your juices spilled across the floor. I was peaceful until you crossed my fence.

I threw a sharp, right uppercut to the tank on Zebb's back; it barely fazed him—just seemed to piss him off—but before he could jump off and get to me, I laid full force with everything I had—all 186 pounds of it—into him with a straight right punch square on his temple that knocked him off Zebb and onto the ground. He was big enough that I needed him to stay down. I swiftly made my way to him and dropped my knee on his chest, causing him to gasp for air. I gave a solid jab right to the mouth, and several blows that were aimed directly for his nose, but he moved while trying to guard himself, and one found his lower jaw. He rolled over and bucked me off as he rose to his knees. I took the opportunity to slip around his back, glide my forearm across his throat, and grab my bicep to secure the choke. I just wanted to let him know that this was going to stop one way or the other, and he wasn't getting up. His eyes rolled back in his head, and I lowered his motionless body onto the hardwood. One of the others in the crew was still pounding on Zebb's head; another had Zebb in a chokehold that looked quite effective; Zebb had come to and was trying to gather his composure, but was struggling to get free of the hold. I assumed this was not the other guy's first fight, and Zebb was getting weaker by the second; veins poked out of his skull from the blood being cut off to his cranium. I grabbed my empty beer bottle off the bar and plowed it over the crewmember's skull. Glass shattered, his grip released on Zebb's throat, and his body crashed onto the blood-stained hardwood. Zebb got to his feet. The kid who had started this whole mess with his loud mouth began to struggle to his feet, he and Zebb squared off against each other. They stood two feet apart, out of breath, both faces seeping blood out of their wounds. Zebb nodded toward the kid as the kid, bent over and trying to catch his breath, steadily looked at Zebb. He spat a fat blood loogie at his feet. "You are still a big, fat, lying fucking ogre." Zebb shook his head in disgust.

The bartender, who hadn't been motivated to remove himself from behind the bar and intervene, hollered out, "You fucking roughnecks. Get the hell out my bar!" Zebb and I looked at each other and had no response. So much for his "Roughnecks Welcome" sign. The bartender reached below the bar and pulled out a sawed-off twelve gauge. The whole place was trashed and mostly cleared out except for us, the kid and his crew, a couple of onlookers, and the extremely pissed bartender holding us at gunpoint. We had overstayed our welcome. We swiftly left as requested, bolting out the front door as we heard the sound of sirens starting to round the corner. Not willing to wait to see if they were for us, we jumped into Zebb's '92 Toyota Tacoma—strange for a 6' 2" man to have such a small truck—but this was no time for jokes, so I held my tongue as Zebb lit up a Marlboro. However, I almost couldn't help myself from laughing as he ground the gear into first and turned his blackened bloody face to me and gave me a smile, showing off his two missing front teeth.

. . . .

I never asked Zebb if the story he'd told was true. Personally, I didn't want to know and kind of had my doubts, as the young roughneck had, but I took it for what it was worth. We hadn't talked since about that wild episode, but I did hear a rumor that he tried to go back to the Middle East and was told he wasn't welcome for some strange reason. Apparently, though, North Dakota had no problem taking him in.

CHAPTER 11
Present Day, Back in Hotel

A persistent knock sounded on my door, and then came the sound of an all-to-familiar voice, way too loud, and way too early after a night shift. "Come on, whipper-snapper, we got work to do."

I looked over at my half-empty bottle of Jack and shook my head, trying to open my eyes. I thought about replying, but more than anything I wanted to hurl the whiskey glass at the door and have it shatter as a warning to go the hell away, but I had a feeling it wouldn't put a great start to the day for me or Zebb.

I yelled the only thing I could think of to buy me some time and let me shake off some sleep. "Gimme a minute!"

"I'm counting." I heard Zebb's laugh of pure joy. It irritated the hell out of me.

"Screw off!" I rolled over and looked at a large, red-letter clock that read 1:27 p.m., and I thought about what I did for a living, wondering if I was really ready to be back. I had gotten to sleep around 9 a.m. after talking to Bryant, having four bourbons, and getting settled in my room. Four hours and some change of sleep and four shots of whiskey—that used to be all I needed for a week sometimes, but I wasn't in the groove anymore. I wiped the crust out of my eyes as Zebb's foot banged against the door.

"Come on, sunshine! Minute's up!"

I rose out of bed—as if I had a choice—and dragged my naked body into a pair of long johns. "Just a fucking minute!" The same laughter sounded out, and I took my time and flipped the coffee pot on before unlocking the door and letting the giant through.

"What in the hell is so important to wake me after being up almost two fucking days?" Zebb stood there wearing a big grin. I couldn't contain my surprise. "You got teeth?"

"Of course I got teeth, you asshole." Zebb retorted as he let himself in.

"I just figured you for a guy that wouldn't have spent the money on them."

"Fuck you." It was the warm welcome I expected from him.

He glanced over to the bottle of Black Label Jack sitting on the dresser as he made his way through the room. I wandered around trying to remember where I put my boots. Zebb pointed at the bottle and teased, "Whoa, whoa, buddy. What happened here?"

I sat on the edge of the bed and struggled to get my socks on. I leaned over, picked up the bottle, and tilted it toward him. "Want some?"

He took the bottle and sat it back on the desk. "I better pass, good buddy. I remember the last time we started drinking that shit. Plus, Bryant would have our asses for showing up with Jack Daniel's on our breath—especially if we didn't share." I knew it to be true.

"You actually thought about it for a second didn't you, you damn drunk. I was only kidding," I spouted.

"Fuck off and get dressed. Let's get to work, Wyatt. We got to get tools ready."

"Can't y'all get fishing tools together without me?"

"You're the only one that's been out on location; we need well info from you."

"I gave all that to Bryant on my way home." The coffee was ready, and I poured some liquid fuel and tilted the pot toward him.

"Yeah, I'll take a cup. I guess I didn't get the memo on that info." He thought about it for a moment before he continued. "Well, you're up now, might as well make yourself useful and head up to the shop to help gather tools." He took a sip of his brew, and neither his eyes nor his words offered any sympathy for me, which I expected. "Seems like you been out of the game for a little while. There ain't no rest for the wicked, Wyatt. Get your boots on and let's go."

I shook my head in disbelief at the suggestion. Out the window, I could see snowflakes starting to drop, and I really just wanted to go back to bed. I situated a blue Carhartt beanie over my skull, slid into a pair of coveralls and pondered the start of a day. I never liked the lack of sleep, but what choice did I have? There was no plaque on my wall granting me sleep at night, and I didn't want one. I knew the life I had chosen, and it was time to put my big-girl pants on and go to work. I felt the fuzzy imbalance between my ears from the whiskey of the morning and the drain from the lack of sleep, I pondered on what life could have been like if I had actually gone to college or at the very least paid attention in high school.

. . . .

I opened the passenger door to Zebb's Dodge and McDonald's cups and coke cans came spilling out. I glanced down at the fast-food bags covering the floor board and a half-eaten cheeseburger sticking out of a Big Mac box. "Zebb, you gonna clean up this pigsty?" I threw my coat in the back and stomped the Big Mac box, watching in disgust as rotten burger squished underneath my Redwings as I slid in.

"You could always drive your own. Well, that probably wouldn't be very legal right now, would it?" He chuckled as he said it, knowing he had me pinned.

"Screw you." I felt the warmth on my behind as I squirmed and kicked my way around the fast-food trash on the floorboard. "Seat heaters ain't half bad, though."

"Yeah, got Bryant to upgrade me from my old truck."

"Right on."

"I gotta stop for fuel; plus, it will give you some time to wake up and kick that hangover."

I leaned my head back, pulled my beanie over my eyes, and tried to rest. "Whatever."

I popped some mints I found in Zebb's console as he fueled and wondered if my drinking would someday be my demise or, at the very least, the end of my career. I wondered how I had made it this far sometimes. In spite of the obstacles and struggles an oilfield life brought, it still had a way to bring you through; you just had demons to battle that never seemed go away.

We parked at the shop and sat for a second watching the snow fall as the wind took it with its own free will. The snow continued piling up, with neither one of us really wanting to get out of the truck. I looked at him and he at me as we both sipped coffee, and I popped a fresh mint and glanced at the thermometer; the needle held steady at 25 degrees.

"Got one coming in," Zebb said.

"Yep." I sipped my coffee and noted the darkening clouds that signaled a cold front coming through. "I suppose we ought to get out of this truck before Bryant looks out that window and sees the two laziest tool hands in the world sitting in the parking lot watching snow and drinking coffee."

He pointed toward me as he spoke. "I suppose. You first."

"I think I'll finish my coffee on second thought."

"Me too." We both chuckled at our lack of ambition.

"So, Zebb, what do you think?"

"I try not to; it gets me in trouble."

"No, really, what do you think we should do about that well?"

"Aw, hell, just run wireline down there and back the damn thing out and jar it out like normal with a spear on the end of the string. I'm thinking Bryant is worried too much about this damn pressure."

"I'm telling you, Zebb, there's something not right about the way its acting."

"Yeah, maybe so, but if you get some fifteen-and-a-half pound or whatever you were going to put downhole, you should be fine. Even so, weight up until you're good. Or find you a good old snubbing unit and just run in with a spear and some jars and fish the damn thing. I'm telling you, it's simple."

"Yeah, I suppose, but I really want to see that pressure gone before we start fishing."

He looked at me, frustrated by my argument. "Fuck it, Wyatt. We fish under pressure all the time. Why are you making such a big deal out of it?"

"I'm telling you, man, this is different. It would go away, then come back, go away, then come back—something is off."

"All right, I'll admit it is a little strange, but it's still just pressure. Let's just get out there and see what the hell is going on. I'm a believer that you have to be on location to get the feel of things before you make a call on a wellbore, but I do trust your judgment. If you say it's trying to kill you, then let's get out there and figure it out."

"I was thinking, you on days, me on nights—what do you think?" I always preferred the older hand to be on days, especially with an older company man. It just worked out better in my experience. Besides, nights were quieter.

He bent his mug to his lips for a sip. "Yeah, sounds good to me." Grabbing the door handle and pushing it open against the wind, he stepped out, crunching the snow beneath his boots. The wind tried to blow his beard away as he smiled toward me. "Come on, Wyatt, it's like jumping in cold water; you just got to do it." I sipped my coffee and gave him a smile, opened the door and reached back for my coat as the wind kicked up, slamming the door into the back of my legs. I grabbed the coat while pushing the door back hard, wanting to knock it off its hinges and bury it in a ditch due to the assault. The chill of the wind iced the tips of my fingers as we made our way through the front door. I lagged behind Zeb as Bryant stepped from his office and met us at the top of the stairs.

"Y'all are about two of the laziest tool hands I have ever met." I figured he had seen us screwing off, drinking coffee and watching snowflakes fall.

While I gathered my bearings, Zebb had a comeback. "What's worse, the ones screwing off or the one watching them screw off?" There was validity in it, though I'm not sure if Bryant agreed with or not; his face showed little amusement.

"Get your asses up here into the boardroom. We got Rikki up here; he wants to go over our plan for fixing this well." There was no more laughter. I sobered up and swiftly stepped up the last couple of stairs behind Zebb. Sitting at the boardroom table, Rikki pored over the well drawing stretched out in front of him that had been taken down from our white board.

I made my way in and shook his paw. "How's it going, Rikki?"

"It's going." He seemed more respectful away from the rig, at least not as much of a stick in the mud, for whatever it was worth. "What's your thoughts on this whole situation, Wyatt?"

"There's a lot to consider, but I'm thinking we should definitely get this pressure under control, and then try to jar it out." We stood there looking at the well diagram as Bryant and Zebb, with pen and paper, took their seats at the round table. Rikki filled Bryant in on details and his thoughts on what should be done and gave us the update on the well. The pressure had gone away. I sketched out a drawing in my tally book of a well bore with stuck pipe and jotted some notes.

Zebb wasn't shy to get into business. He spoke up and asked the question that lingered on my mind. "What mud weight you got in there now?"

"Still got that thirteen-and-a-half pound."

"And it's dead?"

"Yeah, nothing. We figured just leave it be, our drilling engineer doesn't want to waste the money on fifteen-and-a-half pound mud."

Zebb then revealed one of his best traits, which was getting to the point. "I don't think I would be too worried about the money near as much as I would someone's life, or for a lesser matter, a lawsuit of negligence. For Pete's sake, from the sounds of it, you damn near killed Wyatt out there."

Rikki folded his arms as he spoke. "Whatever. It all worked out, and I can't override that engineer, they pretty much call the shots nowadays." You could see Rikki was getting frustrated. He seemed like a child who couldn't get his way due to his own ignorance about how the world actually worked.

Zebb leapt up and pounded his balled fist into the table as his stare dug into Rikki. "The hell you can't! People's lives are on the line. Get him on the phone. I'll override his ass!" Zebb took a seat and straightened the crinkles of denim in his shirt. Everyone in the room and everyone else in the oilfield knew we couldn't do a thing to override the engineer if he was dead set on it. The only thing we could do is turn down the job if we really felt that it was that serious, and it took a set of real balls to turn down a fistful of cash. Usually, you just let them fiddle around until they realized you were there to help.

Rikki stared angrily at Zebb, infuriated at the utter lack of respect. "Call him if you want!"

"He's your engineer, you fucking call him!" Zebb retorted back.

I pushed the conference phone toward Rikki, and he turned his foul glance toward me and started dialing. The speaker rang. I wondered how this would go; I hoped for a little entertainment if Zebb got any resistance.

The ringing stopped and a youthful voice came over the speaker. "This is Dan."

Rikki answered. "Hey Dan, this is Rikki, I'm here with Bryant, Zebb, and our tool hand Wyatt from Anderson Oil Tools."

"All right, what can I do for you?"

Zebb spoke up. "Dan, this is Zebb Morgan here in Williston." Zebb waited respectfully for a reply.

"Yes, how's it going?"

"Going good. We are sitting here with Rikki and Wyatt discussing options on how to proceed with this well and was curious if you would like to join us?" Zebb's voice carried a force that was controlled but precise; there was a demand for respect that would not be denied even when talking to the man who could dismiss us off the job at a moment's notice.

I pictured Dan sitting back in his chair sipping yuppie tea looking at the engineering degree plaque that hung on his wall as he spoke. "Yeah, I would be curious on your thoughts on the situation, Zebb." I quietly wondered if he had any thoughts of his own to offer.

The pressure in Zebb's forehead seemed to lessen as he sensed some headway being made. "I would like to weight up to fifteen-and-a-half pound mud before we do anything else. I believe Wyatt and Bryant will back me on this being the best thing to do before we go any further." I watched as the veins on his forehead started to retract as the pressure eased now that he was making his concerns known.

"I suppose, but there hasn't been any pressure for the last several hours. I'm thinking thirteen point five pound is good enough."

Zebb was calmer than expected with his reply. "I just don't see the issue on covering our ass and yours with fifteen-and-a-half pound mud. If this is acting how Rikki and Wyatt have been saying, then you might be dealing with a whole different situation than just pure gas pressure." His thoughts had a solid foundation and his concern was genuine—nobody wanted to be hurt, nobody wanted to see anyone get hurt, and damn sure nobody wanted to lose a well or it would hurt us all.

"Yeah, possibly, but you have to realize the expense of weighting up and the pain in the ass to put a well into production with heavy fluid in it."

"Well, no offense, but I don't give a shit. If things don't start going our way, this well won't ever be put in production." It was the simple truth, and I could tell Zebb's eyes weren't lying about truly not giving a shit. That was one of the beautiful things about being a tool hand—the money didn't cloud your thinking. Your only concern was in getting a job done successfully, so the oil company could make money down the road off their well.

"You think it's that serious?" Zebb glanced over at me with disbelief on his face. I could see he was holding back, he really didn't want to be an ass, but I could sense he was about to pop off thoughts that coursed through his mind about engineers.

"Yes, Dan, I really do think it's that serious. All of us here agree on this." Bryant hadn't said a damn thing, but it wasn't out of character for Zebb to speak for a whole room in order to reinforce his theory and push his point. I had to admit it was a convincing tactic to pin four opinions against one, especially one that sat almost 700 miles away.

A heavy sigh came over the line as he responded. "Well, I suppose go ahead and weight it up." Dan must have sensed that he had been beaten by over 70 years of downhole experience between three tool hands.

"Will do. Just wanted to talk it over with you."

"Thank you, Zebb. I appreciate your thoughts, and I'm with you on pulling out all the stops for safety. It seems like every time we think we get a step ahead on this well, we take two more back. Whatever we gotta do to get this well done right, let's do."

I watched as Zebb sat back quietly in his cushioned roller chair and let the reply resonate with Rikki. "All right then, to give you a heads up, we were planning to run in there with a screw-in sub and jarring assembly and try to get some muscle on that packer before we start getting fancy. We feel it's the lowest risk and most cost effective."

Dan asked, "Does that packer have a shear point?" I wondered if Zebb would have an answer; he went quiet and looked over at me.

"I'm going to hand that over to my relief; he's got more experience dealing with these HD packers."

"Hey, Dan, this is Wyatt. There is no additional safety or shear on these HD packers; it's just a straight pick up to release." Bryant nodded at me with a sense of satisfaction, and I began to think this might actually work between Zebb and me. Maybe Bryant did know what he was doing in putting us together.

"Gotcha, sounds like a plan. Let's just get this son-of-a-bitch out of the hole." He most likely didn't have a real clue what we were talking about because it wasn't what he dealt with on a regular basis, and to be honest, it really wasn't his job, it was ours. It was hard to hold too much against him; that's why he paid us.

"Will do, boss," Zebb replied. With that, it was settled. Dan hung up, and the line went silent. Zebb gazed at Rikki with a steady glare and gave him a little smirk. "I guess let's weight up, then."

There was no argument that could hold water for

Rikki. Zebb just convinced his boss and completely overrode Rikki's authority. I glanced across the table at Rikki; he was ashen with shame. He stood up with fists clinched so tight that the knuckles had gone white, and he slammed them onto the table. His face was as red as Thanksgiving beets. "WELL, I GUESS SINCE Y'ALL ARE RUNNING THE SHOW, WEIGHT THE MOTHERFUCKER UP!" He turned and stormed out of the room without another word. I looked over at Zebb, and Zebb looked at Bryant—all three of us wearing wicked grins.

Bryant sneered, "Good job, Zebb." I just shook my head and chuckled at the sarcasm from Bryant. We all knew we needed to weight up, it had to be done. It was the only common-sense thing to do. It just didn't agree with Rikki—and the fact that Zebb had made a fool out of him—I couldn't totally blame the guy for being pissed; I would have been pissed too. Nevertheless, there was still a warm chuckle floating deep in my gut from seeing Rikki get overridden.

CHAPTER 12
6 p.m., Same Day: Headed to Rig Site.

The sun was setting behind me; my tires tore up gravel as I took a slight right, putting a dust cloud in my wake. I glanced at the fracking location that sat off in the distance from our rig; a halo of haze from the steam and exhaust from a crowd of diesel pump trucks hovered over it. My focus switched, and my eyes locked onto the faded blue and white derrick. I pushed in the stereo knob and killed the country. I always liked to have about five minutes of quiet before I got to location. I felt better prepared, my mind felt clearer, and I could run through different scenarios and tool options. I needed to catch my bearings before I pulled onto location. I still felt the sluggishness that coffee couldn't mask; my mind was wired but needing sleep—living on borrowed time. Zebb was already there, and I noticed the wireline truck in front of the rig getting set up and a wireline hand stretching wire from the spool. I kept an eye out for Zebb, but I figured he was probably inside the truck's quarters getting together with the wireline engineer and prepping for the back off. I noticed other hands getting explosives ready. I always liked sending explosives downhole. There was something godlike about the possibility of blowing something up down there and manipulating power far superior than you to your advantage and having it work for you. In this case, they had better work for us or we would be in quite a predicament.

I backed the long bed in alongside the shacks, slipped my hard hat on, and went on my hunt for Zebb. Making my way to the front of the rig, I noticed him talking things over with the wireline engineer outside of the truck. There was mention of prima cord and string shots and gathering a plan on how and what connection we wanted to back off above our stuck packer. This wasn't my first back off, but there wasn't a doubt in my mind that Zebb had probably done at least a thousand more than me, so I didn't interrupt, I just listened. Their plan sounded like the silent one running through my mind.

"You boys gonna get this shit done or what?" It was Rikki poking his nose in the business he'd already hired out. Zebb looked him over from head to toe and, without saying a word, turned back to his conversation with the engineer.

Rikki turned toward me. "So, Wyatt, what the hell we going to do here?" I had to hand it to the guy. He wasn't a total fool; he was smart enough to know what he didn't know, and even smarter for not trying to attempt things on his own. I knew it took him eating a slice of humble pie to ask such a dumb question and I respected him for it.

"We're going to back that son of a bitch off and get her out of the hole, simple as that."

"I know that, you moron, but give me a fucking procedure."

I smiled, knowing Zebb and I got on his last nerve, and the sick part of it all is that we enjoyed it. "All right, Rikki. We're going to turn to the right and tighten up that whole drill string, turning her one round to the right for every thousand feet while moving the drill string up and down, allowing torque to work its way through the bends of the well and reaching to each connection." I pointed over to the tools at the edge of the catwalk. "Then, we'll send that string shot downhole with an explosive charge and put it where we want it."

Rikki crossed his arms crossed and soaked up the new information. "All right, then what?"

"We'll put some rounds to the left while holding a slight bit of tension against the stuck point and shoot the charge off using the wireline. That'll cause the box of the connection to heat up and expand and allow the pin to unscrew, and then, Voilà! come out of the hole."

"I gotcha." He seemed satisfied, but I could see from the look in his eyes that he didn't have a clue.

Zebb was intent on ignoring Rikki. His conversation with the wireline engineer had switched to deer hunting and superficial small talk. As long as he didn't have to talk to Rikki, he'd have accomplished his goal. We waited for the rig and wireline guys to get rigged up and ready for us to tighten the string up.

I glanced over and saw one of the wireline hands struggling with the weight bars. The guy was a scrawny fellow who didn't seem to pack much of a punch. I knew it was dog-eat-dog out here in this man's world, and it was sometimes frowned upon to help a hand, but the Good Book tends to frown on not helping your neighbor. "You want a hand with that?"

"Yeah, if you don't mind." I didn't mind a bit. By no means did I want something stupid to happen and either him slip or get busted up. I yanked gloves out of my rear pocket, meandered over, and grabbed ahold of the weight bars with him and helped him haul them over. The weight bars were made of pure tungsten and weighed more than him. I couldn't blame him for struggling. As we grabbed the second one, he looked my way from across the other end of the weight bar.

"Thanks, man. Seems like that wireline engineer thinks he doesn't have to get his hands dirty anymore."

"I don't know if it's so much that as they are both trying to avoid talking to Rikki." I saw a slight smile from him. Anything to ease the situation was a good sign—the less drama we had out here the better.

We sat the weight bar down on a tripod stand and looked up to the rig crew staring down at us from the floor. We heard the words shout from up above we had been preciously waiting for. "We're ready!" I looked at Zebb to verify that he had heard, and indeed he had. I pounced up the stairs as Zebb straggled behind. I loved doing backoffs. There was something neat about singling out one connection out of over 300 and putting explosives downhole, not too much to blow pipe apart but just enough to expand the connection. I looked over my shoulder at Zebb while we climbed. He looked tired. By rights, he had no reason to be; it was me who was hungover and who was going with only a few hours of sleep, but his face sagged and his feet lingered as if it were him. Things seemed to be taking a toll on him—not just this job, but this career. It was the path we had chosen, or it had chosen us—long days with even longer nights. We both knew how fortunate we were to be trading shifts with each other on this particular job. It was an unusual circumstance—most of the time you were iron-manning it for 24 hours no matter how long it took. Most people wouldn't trade a lack of sleep for a paycheck, but it wasn't all about a paycheck. Out here, there was more to it than that to make a man push himself like this—it was a lifestyle. It's what we loved, and it's all we knew. We had the privilege to keep up with all of the latest technology and use it to pull oil out of the hell that holds it while holding a supervisor position—all with no degree, plus money that would put a doctor to shame. It was plain and simple; our job was to make things work downhole no matter how good or bad the design was, no matter how stupid the engineer was that designed it. Most of all, it was our last chance to make something of our lives, our last real chance to not be throwing tongs or latching pipe for the next 30 years, trying to get by. Watching him climb those stairs, I didn't see that drive in him anymore. It was gone. He couldn't hide the fact that he was tired as he climbed one step after the other, making his way to a floor that had built his life, fed his family, and sent his daughters to school. Nevertheless, even though he felt he no longer needed to be there, he still dragged his way up. This field has a way of keeping you around.

His mouth opened with instruction as soon as his Redwings hit the floor. "All right, let's tighten this son-of-a-gun up." Zebb positioned himself and crossed his arms beside Vann in the driller's station. His wrinkled and ragged face carried the seriousness of the situation. It was a relief to have him on site; this was his specialty. Even though I could get it done, I knew Zebb was the prime option. "Let's find that neutral point," he ordered. We watched as Vann came down on the pipe and found weights for Zebb. They were still the same; the indicator needle neutralized at 115K, with 120K up, and 90K down. Vann tightened the 9,800 feet of drill pipe using a simple old formula of one round per thousand feet, giving him close to 10 rounds to play with. Most don't totally grasp why you have to go so many rounds, but it's really simple when you think about it. If you have almost 10,000 feet of drill pipe in a well that bends and twist and has a whole lot of other complex things happening, only God truly knows what is going on down there and you're trying to tighten the whole footage at once, one turn at surface never equals one turn downhole, definitely not at a depth of 9,000+ feet. It's kind of like having a garden hose stretched out across your lawn, if you turn it a half a turn at one end, the other half won't see all of that turn.

I watched as Vann counted rounds and watched torque, slowly moving the drill pipe upward and down to work torque to every connection and watching how many turns released back after releasing torque. It was a tortuous process, but necessary. The string had to be tight or you could back off the wrong connection; the most unstable connection is the one to back off.

He finished tightening and ordered wireline to send down the explosives inside the drill pipe. The engineer double-checked every spec of the charges and sent a guy up on a winch to guide the explosives down inside the drill pipe.

I always enjoyed it when it was time to send explosives downhole. It brought back the memory of when I had to do the same as a roughneck, and my driller, along with my consultant, thought it would be real funny to trick me into picking the short straw so that it was my job to send the explosives down, but right as I was going up, my consultant told me that if I let them touch any iron they would go off 'cause it's a short charge—whatever a short charge was because I had no idea. I remember not being afraid, like they wanted me to be. The fact of the matter was that I could slam the explosives on the derrick leg and it wouldn't make a damn. If they were foolish enough to send a young, divorced roughneck up with enough explosives to blow everyone all to hell, well, they weren't going to make it very long in this business anyhow.

My thoughts were different now, though. I felt more at ease once the explosives started downhole. At least if they went off downhole, it wouldn't blast us all to smithereens. I finally had some things going right in my life; an abrupt end to it wasn't something I wanted.

Zebb and I headed downstairs and entered the cab of the wireline truck. My eyes fixed on the screen inside the cab of the wireline truck as we buried the E-line that held an electrical conductor in the middle of it. It zipped through the drill pipe at over 300 feet a minute pushing the bomb we just sent downhole. Zebb shook off the snow from his boots, seemingly caring more about the soles of his feet than the job at hand. He joined me on the cushioned bench, and we watched from behind the engineer as he continued to drop the wire at over 300 feet a minute downhole while keeping an eye open for any hang ups, any weight change, or anything else out of the ordinary.

Zebb looked my way and demanded, "Pour me some coffee, young'un." I barely responded to the slight; it didn't really bother me. I glanced his direction, grabbed the handle of the pot, and slid it across the cheap, flimsy mica counter-top that provided the semblance of a desk.

"You can pour it yourself." I was simply not pouring his coffee; it was a line not to be crossed. It's one thing to ask a man for a pot of coffee, but totally another to be told to pour it. The only way I was pouring his coffee would be in his boots.

His eyes wrinkled and crinkled as he smiled over at me. "It's like that, huh."

"Yep, it's like that." I knew to watch Zebb. The phrase *give him an inch, he'll take a mile* was invented because of guys like Zebb. Today I'm pouring coffee, tomorrow he would want me to wash his truck and who knows what else. See how much the man next to you will give and you can take a little bit more. We were setting boundaries at that moment. It would have been one thing if nobody were around, but demanding that a man pour your coffee in front of others while you're fully capable was tantamount to wearing a wig and being another man's bitch in prison. He poured himself a cup, all the while giving me a smile. I enjoyed working with the older fishing hand, but he usually tried to get the best of you.

"Here put that back up, young'un." I pushed the pot back onto the burner. He could have that one. Boundaries had been set, and there was no reason to be rude. He held a smirk on his lips as he sipped his coffee and nodded to me as he made a tight fist and edged it out toward me. I gave him a healthy fist bump and smirked back at him. It was a strange world out here at times. Every little thing mattered, every ounce of respect was fought for, nothing was given. It seemed small, but as a tool hand you had to hold your own whether it was a million dollar decision or a cup of coffee. You went off of nothing but reputation and respect, and no man gave it to you, you took it, even when it came in the slightest of forms.

I watched as the digits on the screen creeped to 9,000 feet; every connection in the drill pipe displayed on the screen in the form of extended lines.

"Come on up to 8870 feet and tighten the line, so we can see the connections," I said. The engineer asked no questions and simply reeled the line back in one hundred thirty feet, thus putting our tools on the connection that would hopefully back off for us. "Print that out," I said as Zebb just sat relaxed on the back bench sipping coffee. I listened to the printer start to crackle and spit out a chart that resembled a heartbeat scan. The solid lines stretching the page were the indicating factor of identifying the connections of drill pipe. I circled the connection that sat dead on the money at 8870 feet; this would leave one joint of drill pipe to fish. I handed the sheet over to Zebb, who seemed content as he bent the Styrofoam to his lips and took a sip.

"Whatta you think?" I asked. He took the paper and tapped his foot as he took another sip. He studied the chart, placing his fat, oversized ogre finger where I had just circled.

"Looks good. Let's shoot it."

The wireline engineer's face brightened. "That's the best thing I heard all day."

I heard the crack of Zebb's voice behind my ear spit out instruction. "Zero everything and get your depths and corrections right and let me know when you're ready and check up on the floor and make sure all that torque is staying steady."

I picked up the radio and checked with the driller.

His response came back. "Yep, left-handed torque is still in there."

"Good."

The engineer rotated his dial and armed the explosives and looked at me. "Ready?" I looked back at Zebb, and he gave us the slight nod of an old sage.

I watched the thinnest hand on my watch tick as I waited for it to round the twelve. "Shoot!" I said as we watched the gauges and waited for an indication at the same time shooting glances up to the floor. I clocked 15 seconds, collar locator spiked, we watched drill pipe on the floor start spinning with fury to the left.

We heard a voice on the radio scratch out, "It went! We are officially out!"

Zebb, the engineer, and I exchanged smiles. It had worked. You just had to have that touch. The precision of a surgeon, but the mind of a roughneck. You just gotta feel it.

CHAPTER 13
*9 P.M.: Back off completed and Tripping out of the hole
(Top of Fish = 8870 feet)*

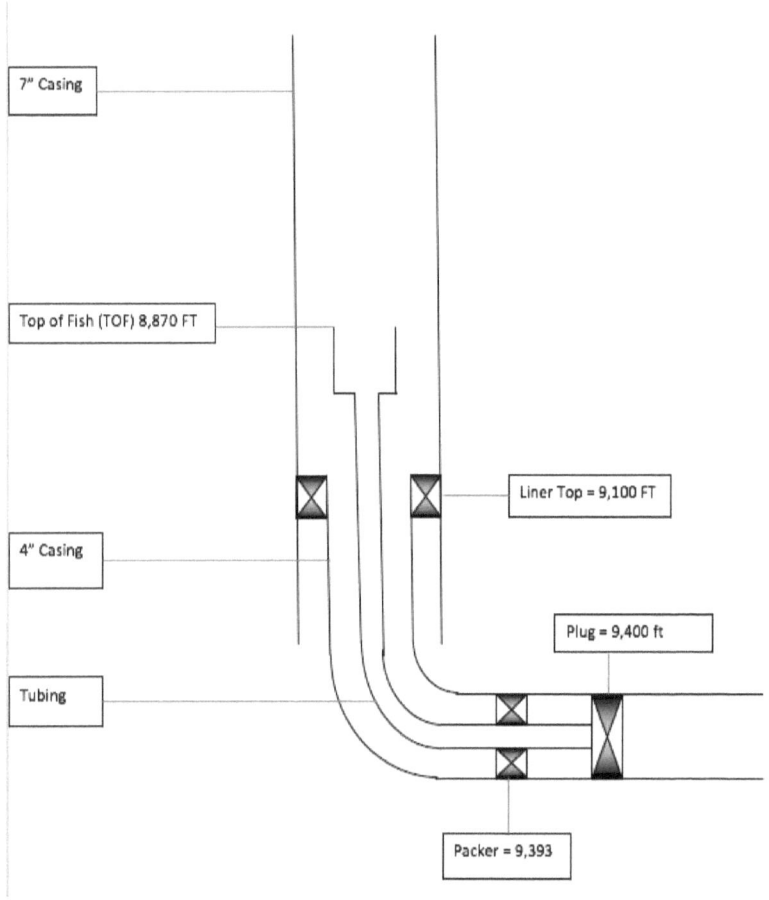

"What's our options now?" Rikki asked as Zebb and I entered his trailer trailing after him. The three of us stood looking at one another in the midst of a short consultation.

Zebb sipped his coffee as he sat in the chair next to Rikki. "Right now, we got two good options and a third one, not so good."

"Remind me what two those are."

"One, run a screw-in sub with oil jars up above and screw into the fish downhole and try to jar it out. Or two, we could run a spear with a set of jars."

Rikki sat in thought, and for a second I thought I heard echoes sounding in the hollowness between his ears. These were standard procedures he should have known. "What's the third?"

"The third is a route you don't want go."

"Maybe so, but what the hell is it?"

"We would have to get lower to the packer and mill over it with a washover shoe, something you absolutely want no part in right now."

"It's something worth considering."

Zebb looked over at me in disbelief, which I was sure washed over my face as well. It was insane to even continue this conversation. It would be the absolute worst choice in the history of oil wells, but I was starting to wonder if it might be what we would do.

"Yeah, we could do that." Zebb sipped his coffee, not giving a damn about going the stupid route. If Rikki wanted to make this job stretch out for another couple of months, I had a feeling that Zebb would let him, and Zebb and I would just keep pocketing the cash. But was it moral? "We could always call your engineer," I said, but I had a feeling that Rikki probably would never call that engineer again with Zebb in the room.

Rikki looked at Zebb and respectfully asked, "What do you want to do?"

"I wanna run a screw-in sub, get screwed in and start

jarring, but if you want to washover, I won't stop you. After all, it is your well."

Rikki nodded in agreement as he spoke. "Let's get screwed in, then."

Zebb sat his coffee down, clapped his hands together in applause, and congratulated Rikki. "Good choice."

Rikki's face seemed to boil from the blood underneath as he responded, "Look here, you fuckheads! I sense your sarcasm; you couple of smartasses but I truly want y'all to understand that this is my well! Y'all are here just to help me. Y'all are just the help! Got it?" He stared us down to sink the point deep in our bones. I wasn't sure if it was the clapping that irritated him or if it was just our presence and the fact that we breathed the same quality air as him.

"Oh, yeah, we got that, Rikki. Anything else you would like to inform us of?" I was glad Zebb could think of something to say. I still wondered why somebody who was supposed to be so in charge had to keep reminding himself and everyone else that he was, in fact, in charge.

He looked directly at me and responded, "I think that's it, but y'all need to understand it."

I couldn't believe that he was looking at me and not Zebb. "Yes, sir," I said. As soon as I said it, I realized that it came out with a hint of sarcasm that I hoped he wouldn't catch.

He caught it and glared at me. "How come every time you say 'Yes, sir' it sounds like 'fuck you'?" What do you say to a mad man? He interprets everything as "fuck you."

"Are we going to sit around here and circle jerk everything and worry about your emotions or are we going to go back to work?" Zebb asked. Rikki stared at us as we stood there like two puppy dogs needing discipline for something that we didn't even know we did. He finally waved his hand, giving us a brusque snort of dismissal, as though he were a king perched on his throne. "Get the hell out of here."

"Yes sir," Zebb spouted. We made a beeline for the exit. My hand hit the metal door with a force I hadn't meant and slapped the frame.

Rikki's head flashed back out the door almost as soon as it slammed behind us. "Don't slam my fucking door!"

"Yes, sir!" As I said it, Zebb smiled at me. It was all so childish, and I felt stupid for stooping to his level. He probably got some sort of sick kick out of it all. How he had made it to his position, and who put the knucklehead in charge, I had no clue, but I sure wouldn't have minded meeting the son of a bitch. There was a pile of really good consultants, and we ended up with the true jackass of the group. The sad thing was that it seemed more common nowadays.

As Zebb and I neared his truck, and I entered the passenger seat, I looked over to him. "Why in the hell do you think he's like that?"

"He's insecure."

"Insecure about what? The son of a bitch is in charge."

"Exactly. He feels out of control; he doesn't know what he's doing. We are here, and his knowledge just doesn't match up."

"I suppose."

Zebb leaned against the Dodge as we looked at the wireline crew packing up and getting ready to leave. Meanwhile, the rig kept pulling drill pipe from the core of the earth. We watched in silence as we soaked up the situation.

"What you thinking?" I asked. It was a logical question, and I couldn't think of a better conversation starter.

"A three-hundred-pound dog is a big son of a bitch."

"Huh?"

"You asked."

"Fair enough." I leaned back on my headrest and figured there was no point in further conversation. We both knew we needed to get the next bottom hole assembly (BHA) ready so that we could screw into the connection downhole and have a set of jars so that we could try to hammer it up hole with our new set of tools once they get out of the hole with the drill pipe. Zebb seemed as ambitious as I did about it all as we sat there watching flakes of snow flutter.

. . . .

11 P.M.

"You hold her, and I'll screw her," Zebb remarked as we screwed crossovers together to be run on the bottom of our jars. I couldn't help but smirk as I held tightly onto our set of jars and Zebb spun the crossovers on; it was one of the corniest of oil field jokes. The rig was almost out of the hole with the string of pipe. I shifted my hard hat and felt the frigidness on my bare hands from the cold of the steel.

The flakes continued to drift down in the brightness of rig lights on the floor that lite us up. I shifted weight in my boots as I moved forward, leaving an imprint in the ankle-deep snow. My palms felt the snow starting to build on the handrails, each grip reminding me of the mistake I had made in misplacing my gloves. I remembered that the temperature before Zebb and I got out to get the tools ready had read 4 below zero and thought about the stupidity of it. As I made my way up the steel steps to the rig floor, it was dropping fast, and with each degree, I felt the severity of the situation we could possibly be in if this pressure came back to haunt us.

"Chest high or die!" Vann yelled. I watched as Dakotah and slippery Jeff pulled the 200-pound slips out, bringing them clear up to their chest. I liked their spirit. The massive blue and white derrick legs stared me down as my ears clang from the ring of drill pipe being racked back and slamming into one another in the derrick.

"Chest high or die!" I looked over at Vann as he yelled again from the old-fashioned brake handle. With determination in his eye, he pulled the next stand of pipe up as fast as possible; Vann wanted those slips to hit their chest every pull, if for nothing else but his entertainment. The brakes screeched on cue as Vann pushed down on the cold steel of the brake handle and grabbed one more stand as one of the hands clacked the elevators shut around the next tool joint.

"I wanna see you break 'em!" Vann screamed toward the floor. It was every roughneck's goal to try and break a set of elevators, at least every good one. They weighed close to 500 pounds and were solid steel; you were never going to even dent them, much less break them by slamming them closed, no matter how tough you were, but there was always merit in trying that was just the roughneck way.

Zebb stood next to me enjoying the show as his ZZ-Top beard blew in the wind. "They ain't half bad," he said as he nudged me and nodded toward our floor hands slamming the slips down on the rotary.

"Yeah, not half bad."

My eyes followed the drill string up toward the board

where the derrick hand was prepping to pull pipe back. Oh, how I loved it up there when it was my time. I could tell that the hand knew what he was doing; his footing was right, his ropes were tight, and he was at home. Everything was clicking for their trip, and it was a nice sight to see. I recalled the memories etched back in my mind of when that was my home, but I found my mind wandering to the most dangerous time of my life, just a few years back.

. . . .

The note was simple, but my eyes teared as they glazed over it:

I'm sorry, Wyatt, I just can't live with you anymore. We have grown apart, and I have tried to tell you so many times of the things you do wrong. You just won't be the man I need you to be, and I can't be the woman you want me to be. You have changed too much for me to love you any longer. It seems this oilfield has taken you and warped you into somebody I don't know. I know you will look for me, but please don't. I don't want to be with you anymore. I'm going to miss some things about you, but this is for the best.

I had almost expected an "I love you" at the end. That's how all our notes had ended from sophomore year on—notes passed in between classes, sometimes after only not seeing each other for short periods off. I fell to my knees face forward as the pain started to overcome me.

That was it. I just lost my high school sweetheart, my wife, my first love. I collapsed on the cold, carpeted floor with my heart beating out of my chest. My pain was unbearable. I felt it in the core of my bones as every part of me ached with the agony of a breaking heart. Tears streaked my face, and my palms were laced with sweat. I lay there in search of rest without the comfort of so much as a friend. I was done; my life was surely over, my ambition gone with my very being crushed. What was the point? I had toiled so hard to make things work, yet everything I had worked for was out the door with no hope of return. I gasped for air, just one peaceful breath, but none could be found. The pain ran in the depths of my soul far too deep for any peace. I leaned onto the cold floor and closed my eyes.

I was told by many our love had not been real—just puppy love—but what older and wiser individuals can't seem to understand is that puppy love is real to puppies. I'd heard the stories of this happening and was warned of the sharp knife the oilfield could deliver to your marriage. But not to me. It wasn't possible. I had thought this through, planned meticulously left, right, and center; this oilfield was supposed to be our way out. No more searching an empty change jar for grocery money—no more! This was our ticket out. How could I have screwed it all up? What did I miss? I had no idea our ticket out was my ticket into a new kind of hell that I wasn't sure would ever cease. I shouldn't have been mad. Who could blame her? I worked night and day. If there was an extra shift, I took it, no questions asked. That rig had become my life. I worked the derricks more than I worked my home. It was the only place I felt at home. Even though she begged me to leave, I couldn't. I was drawn like a moth to a flame.

My eyes opened, but the pain remained. My heart felt as if it had erupted, and I could not raise myself off the floor. "Jesus, how could you let this happen? How can it be? We went to church. We tried our very best to go every Sunday. We trusted you, and this is how you repay me? I loved her. She was my all, my everything, and you took her. It's you who's in control, after all. Right? So you did it, you took her, but she wasn't yours to take."

It wasn't a prayer that I said, it was blame, pure blame. I tried to muster some strength, but there was none. I was done, crushed to my very core, officially finished. I crawled over and lifted myself to my knees and screamed for mercy in a single AAAAAAARRRHHHHH! I felt a brief release as I kneeled there for what seemed like hours, slumped over the foot of the couch where we had sat together so many nights before.

My eyes soaked the cushions in tears. I recouped myself, wiped my eyes, and quietly asked God for forgiveness for me blaming Him.

Two weeks later, 20 years old, I stood on a board 94 feet up from a rig floor in the dark of the night on a rig that had raised me as much as any family. I stood there an experienced derrick hand, trained in my trade, staring at the very ground that could end my pain. I looked at the stump of drill pipe and thought about it piercing through my chest and the sick feeling of how good it would feel to just get it over with, to terminate the pain. I thought of the last stand of drill pipe I latched being the very tool of my death. I thought of my newlywed/divorced roughneck blood spilling everywhere as my body rested on the very floor I was so committed to serving. Maybe that's what I deserved. I thought of my crew having to pick up what was left of my body off the floor as they washed my blood into the gutters that waited along the edge of that cold steel floor. All I would have to do is drop my belly belt, undo my lanyard and take the fall. I wished someone was there to push me; it could all be over. I couldn't stop staring; my eyes felt locked, dry from a lack of blinking. It seemed like the first time they were dry in weeks. My mind was struggling as I stared forward in a trance and saw a dark, deserted soul standing on the elevators in front of me. His finger stretched out toward me, and the fierceness of the hatefulness of his possessed face made my heart go cold as it spoke. "Just do it! Get it over with. You're worth nothing. Look at you, you're worthless! Just Jump! I own you, Wyatt!" I didn't know who this creature was or why I felt a sudden loss of control as I unclipped my lanyard, pushed the drill stand aside and started unbuckling my belly belt.

"Kleinfield!" It was Jeremiah on the radio.

"Kleinfield! Pick up the fucking radio!"

I snapped back, startled out of my fixation. Maybe it was the fact that only my father ever used my last name, and that was only when things got really serious or when I was ready to do something real stupid.

I stared at the set of elevators awaiting the stand of drill pipe I had just set aside, and the radio cracked over again. "Wyatt! You all right up there? You want me to send someone up there to you?"

I closed my eyes and whispered to myself, "You are a child of God. Don't forget it." As the words left my lips and I opened my eyes, I noticed the creature was gone, and I felt a peace overwhelm me. Everyone down below was looking up at me. I sincerely hoped no one knew of the evil that had just crossed my path. I wondered if they saw the same creature I saw or wondered if I was crazy. I picked up the radio. "No, sir, just had to get my bearings." I grabbed the strap of my belly belt and stretched it tight and buckled it even tighter.

"Well, get 'em, and lock 'em in! Only twenty-five left to latch and we can go home for the night!"

I thought about the darkness that had entered my mind. Only 25 more until home. Who cared about home? It was the last day of the hitch, and home was the last thing I wanted. I felt incarcerated; this was the only life I knew, and I couldn't cope with any other. I was already home.

SLAM! I crashed the stand of drill pipe into the elevators and grabbed ahold of the horns of the elevators as if my hands were wrapped around a lion's throat. CLACK! Right then I knew I would make it through this, come hell or high water. I pushed my emotions aside and slammed every one of the last 25. I tried to demolish the pipe. I wanted to destroy those elevators. I wanted to make them feel what I felt. I wanted that iron to beg for mercy just as I had.

I latched the 25th stand and came down. There was no sweet talk from my buddies on the floor or any compassion. Not that they didn't have any, but I believe they just didn't know what to say. It was clear what had been on mind while I was up there. They simply tipped their hard hats to me, just glad to have me back on the ground. They weren't fools, and they were no better than me. We did everything with a passion, as though every day was our last day. Loving was no different, and because of it, I had almost experienced my last day.

I hung up my harness. Jeremiah was quiet, consumed in a well control book until I entered the doghouse, and he simply looked up and straight into me with a heart of gold showing in his eyes. "You scared me up there. Keep your head and things will get better."

"How do you know?"

"Just trust me." I did trust him, like a big brother. Anything he had ever told me about a rig or a well proved true. I had no reason to doubt him; his track record was clean with me.

. . . .

My thoughts cleared and came back into focus as the final joint of drill pipe came out of the hole, and I heard Zebb's voice bellow, "Throw that hole cover on!"

The joint looked good for having just been charged with explosives. Back offs have almost become a lost art due to the new technology; a lot of drilling companies would rather drill around something than get it out of the hole.

"Look at that, young'un, perfect back off." Zebb prodded me in the ribs as he joked. He truly seemed to think he was God's gift to the oilfield. "Eight thousand, eight hundred and seventy feet of pipe down there, with over two hundred and eighty connections, and I pinpointed that one." He chuckled to himself.

"Now if you could only become humble," I said. He shot me a glare while still splitting the chuckle.

"Yep, don't see that happening anytime soon."

"Me neither." I glanced at him and saw the tired flowing from his eyes as I glanced at the hour hand of my watch. It was starting to round midnight.

"Why don't you go and get some sleep and let me get

these tools downhole?" I said.

"I wanna be up here when we screw into that fish."

"Fair enough. I'll get you up."

"Will you bring me breakfast too?"

"Go fuck yourself."

He laughed, placed a hand on my shoulder, and spoke with a trace of seriousness. "You sure you got this, kid?"

"Yeah, I got her. Get the hell outta here."

He nodded and headed off to conk out in the backseat of his truck and get what little semblance of sleep he could. I was still functional, even though I felt the syrup starting to enter my brain.

CHAPTER 14
Midnight

My mind focused back on business as I glanced toward Dakotah. "Let's drag that drill collar up here and pick up tools."

I heard the infamous clack of the elevators slamming shut around the sub on top of the collar from a hand who meant business as I checked my numbers. Vann raised the drill collar, suspending it in the air while awaiting our assembly to be installed underneath it. My bumper sub and jars followed, swinging through the V-door into the arena of the floor. I nodded toward Dakotah and directed, "Let's get wrenches over here."

The big Sioux nodded, left, and immediately returned moments later with two 48-inch pipe wrenches slung over his massive shoulders that weighed over half my body weight. He grabbed one wrench and threw the other to me as my arms sank in catching it. I grabbed ahold of the wrench, hand-tightening the jars and bumper sub onto the collar. Dakotah brought out the iron roughneck, slapped it on the pipe, wrapped its jaws around the tool joints, torqued the connections, and spiked the gauge.

He grabbed the screw-in sub that sat next to the derrick leg and held up the iron, which I helped him screw underneath the assembly as he torqued connections to spec. I motioned for Vann to bring the string down. Before the screw-in sub disappeared downhole, Dakotah spat a fat loogie on the end. I chuckled and turned to Vann. "All right, she's ready now." Vann just stood looking at me, waiting. True to tradition, I gathered saliva between my gums, hocked the biggest loogie I could muster, and turned back to Vann. "You good now?" He smiled back and nodded as he lowered the assembly into the darkness of the unknown.

Dakotah and I immediately each grabbed a slip handle and threw the 200-lb piece of iron filled with tungsten teeth that bit around the top of the exposed drill collar and then clamped it. We listened to the crunch of tungsten on iron as Vann rested the weight of the short string on the tungsten dies. Dakotah turned around, breathed out a sigh. I watched a long, slinky, clean-shaven boy come up the stairs dressed in oil-stained blue jeans that looked like they'd been worn for at least the last couple of days. He walked across the floor with a swagger right up next to Dakotah and smiled, showing off his missing front tooth.

"Move over Injun. Let Jeffy show you how it's done." He stretched one of his slinky arms out and unlatched the elevators as he looked at me. "Well? What's next, t-o-o-o-l-l-l hand?"

My hand thrust down on the winch lever as I nodded toward the collar rising up through the V-door that he stood in front of. "Better get ready, fl-o-o-r-r hand." I watched his eyes widen in surprise as he turned to see the collar coming full speed toward him. He wrapped his body around the iron as it drug him across the floor, and, with remarkable accuracy, he landed it right into the mouse hole.

He glared at me and then at Dakotah, who stood on the opposite side of the floor. "Now! That's how daddy does it!" I chuckled with him as a smirk split his face.

"Right on. Good job." I waited as they handled the collar and latched elevators around it installed it onto the string, sending it down hole. We brought up five more before confusion hit the floor again.

"What's next, boss?" Dakotah asked.

"Going to winch up that accelerator," I said.

"All right!" Jeff shouted toward us. He grabbed hold of the winch line and pulled the slack out as I lowered the line, all the while yelling to the big Sioux, "Dakotah! Get down there and choke that strap around the accelerator, you big dumb Injun!" I figured Jeff to be a dead man just as soon as that Native American could find him alone. The big Sioux stepped down the forty steel steps to the catwalk and didn't seem the least bit fazed; he just went about his business and strapped the accelerator. When he was finished, he looked upwards and shot us a fat middle finger. Jeff turned toward me and smiled. "That's how you handle those Injuns."

I nodded and smiled. "You will be lucky if he doesn't handle you 'cause I think you just made a new best friend."

"That Injun doesn't have the balls. Don't you know we chop those off before we let them on the rig?" I winched the accelerator up as Jeff tilted his head back and chuckled. "Well, maybe we missed one. It's his first rig; if you can't piss the new guy off, then what are we doing out here?"

"I think you succeeded."

I pushed the handle down to elevate the 12-foot accelerator as Jeff grabbed the iron and mouse-holed, setting slips and removing the winch line and letting it rest while awaiting drill pipe.

Metal grazed metal as Jeff shouldered against the first stand of drill pipe coming from the derrick. Vann roared the engines of the rig to life, raising the stand of drill pipe from the black leg that stood in the derrick. It was one of the slickest sounds on the rig floor due to the feeling of adrenaline that it created. You could feel things coming together to start downhole on a trip to catch a fish.

Jeff stabbed the stand of drill pipe into the box of the accelerator that sat mouse-holed and brought the iron roughneck out, torqueing the connection. Vann raised the stand and landed the accelerator into the drill string and sent it downhole after being torqued. Dakotah made his way back up to the floor to fulfill his duties and replace me on the floor as the trip progressed. I looked down at the grease and drilling fluid that found its way onto my coveralls—disgusting. I was slightly ashamed of myself for being perturbed when I had built a career from swimming in the stuff. I looked up at Vann and noticed him laughing as he watched me look myself over. "Get a little on you?"

"Yep, sure did."

"Damn it."

I chuckled with him. "Such is life, I suppose." I wouldn't have minded near as much if I didn't have to get back to my office. Last thing I wanted was a truck slathered in drilling mud and grease.

I walked over and stood beside him. Vann's focus remained on delivering the top drive up to the waiting derrick hand. I waited for the clack of elevators as the derrick hand slammed them shut around the neck of the drill pipe, and Vann started bringing the stand down to the surface to bury it in to the earth's core.

"Vann, there ain't no speed limit on this baby."

"All right, sounds good. I'll run her."

"All right, let's get to bottom and get this fish out."

"Will do." I turned and walked toward the steel-grated

stairs. My phone buzzed in my pocket; I pulled it out and saw Jessica's name flow across the LED screen. A nice surprise, but strange for her to be calling at midnight. I halted halfway down the stairs, held the phone, and stared at the screen. I wondered what she had to say. Maybe she wondered why she hadn't heard from me; maybe she tried to go in for some BBQ and talked with my boss. I wondered how that might have gone. Four rings flashing her name seemed to last a lifetime while I stood still on the grated stairs staring at the phone. Finally, I took my chances, answered and pressed it to my ear. The chill of the snow found its way onto my neck the second the phone replaced my hardhat liner.

I answered in the most cheerful tone I could muster as I continued down the steps. "Hey there, beautiful! How's it going?"

"You weren't going to tell me that you took the job and skipped town?"

My thoughts were as still as pond water; I could think of nothing to say. You would have thought I could have planned this out better since I had figured this call might come. I had to respond quickly; I realized the late night call meant she probably couldn't sleep due to being so pissed, but I was grasping at straws, and the thought of hanging up and forgetting the whole thing sounded quite good at that moment except it would have been considerably cowardly, so instead I stammered, "Well... Um... I was going to but..." From the silence, I sensed the weakness of my response. She waited. The line sat quiet, the sound of death. I needed something stronger, some thoughtful reason for not calling. "I thought we discussed it at dinner." I said, playing the confused card: not a strong play, but when it's all you've got, it's all you've got. I stepped off the last stair and started over to my truck.

"I don't believe we did. We talked about an opportunity, a second date, and many other things, but never that we wouldn't see each other for God knows how long!" Her voice, brassy but soft as fire rang with conviction that struck my soul. It was as simple as that. I was wrong, and she was right, but I was not admitting that. If I admitted that, I would surely lose every argument from here on out. I wanted to catch her in the worst of ways, worse than anything, worse than I ever wanted to catch any fish downhole. She presented herself in such a fashion that my mind couldn't separate emotions from desire. Maybe it was the way she filled a dark dress snug to the hip, maybe it was that when she walked she held the confidence of a queen; one knew they could hand her the world, and she would return it to you a far better place. Whatever it was, she had it and I wanted it. But I knew that right this very second, I was trapped in a conversation I couldn't get out of. I figured her memory was probably far better than mine, especially considering the inebriated night of our date. The silence seemed deafening and tore me in two. I wondered if I would blow it right that very second. My emotions were running wild for her. The only good thing about the call was that it relayed the fact that maybe she liked me also. I clung to that thought.

I found the courage, if that's what it could be called, to respond. "I had my doubts whether you would really want to know or if you even cared." Maybe it wasn't right to play it back on her, but it was all I had, the oldest trick in the male playbook. However, there was some slight truth to it. Did she really care? Was there anything there? This phone call told me that she, in fact, did care, and I felt like a real piece of work.

"Well, maybe I don't, especially if you don't think enough of me to say goodbye." As her words settled, it felt like a cold blade had pierced my heart.

"I see. But nobody said I was gone for good; I just left in such a hurry." I paused for a second, then continued, "Honestly, you really want to know why I didn't call?"

"That's why I called, isn't it? I honestly would like to know why we had such a good time and then you burn out of town and blow me off. I happened to quite enjoy your company, but when I don't even get a phone call, I'm left with the opinion that you didn't much care for mine."

I felt her pain, her truth, as I tried to recover. "That wasn't it at all. I thoroughly enjoyed your company, but I understand where you're coming from. I realize it wasn't right, but I honestly thought you would say it was over, and there was no chance for us to work, and I just honestly didn't want to hear it. I didn't want the pain." I didn't know what else to say, so I shut up.

"Well, you sure did a lot of figuring on my behalf." It was then that I realized that she wasn't mad, she was simply hurt, rejected and declined by a possible friendship, a possible relationship that could have lasted. I felt her sting because I harbored my own hurt, just not from her.

"Yeah, I suppose I did."

"I don't understand why men seem to think they know everything a woman is thinking."

"Us men, huh? I see, now I get stereotyped."

"Yes, indeed, if you can read my mind, then I can stereotype you." Her tone had changed from anger to a playfulness that was music to my ears.

"I see." I paused to ponder her words. "Why don't we

just see how things play out?" I said, not fully knowing to what I had just agreed.

"I would be fine with that. I'm not totally opposed to having a long-distance relationship, if you're not. I just don't want to hear about you at Whisper's with the boys sticking twenties down some dirty stripper's panties."

I chuckled at her concerns as I walked toward my truck. "I don't think you gotta worry. Let's give it a try and just see where it goes."

"That would be nice. Let's try. What could it hurt?" I wondered if she had ever felt the hurt of a first love. I wondered if she held any scars.

"Where do we start?"

"We just talk. That's all we can do. You tell me about your day, I tell you about mine. We discuss things of importance, things that can change the world around us, whatever comes to mind."

I breathed softly in relief and felt my heart push a boulder off of my shoulders. "That would be nice." I smiled as I felt the wind start to pick up speed and the snow chill my face. We said goodbye with a promise to talk soon. When the call ended, a sense of the day's accomplishments on the job washed over me, but what still needed to be done burdened me. I brushed the snow off of my door handle and reached in the backseat to grab my laptop from the sleeve it rested in and plopped it on my center console. I thought of our well. I thought of the fish downhole we still had to catch. I thought of how that fish had developed on my watch and wondered if I would get blamed for the likes of it. I knew there was nothing I could have done about it, but it was just a matter of whether Rikki's higher-ups agreed with me or not. It was not a question that could be answered right now. My misgivings lingered as I plugged numbers into Excel creating a pipe tally and adding up where we would tag the fish. Out of the corner of my eye, I watched Dakotah make his way step-by-step down the stairs. He looked like a giant coming across a battlefield. He carried a massive 20-pound sledge over his shoulder and walked with determination toward my truck. I started to wonder whether or not he thought me in cahoots with Jeff. I wondered if Jeff was up there dead but quickly remembered that Vann was still operating the top drive, and I could only assume Jeff was still breathing. Drilling rigs don't stop for much but death usually brings them to a screeching halt.

He leaned on my truck with the sledge still over his shoulder and motioned me to roll my window down. I obliged. In a slow voice, he patiently asked, "Did you help Jeff make fun of me while I went down to the catwalk?" His eyes stared into me, waiting for my answer. Half of me wanted to crumble, but I stared back.

"Sure didn't, just guilty by association." I wondered if he would reach in and crush my skull with his mammoth, darkened hands, but he didn't, he just stared into me.

"All right, mister tool hand." His tone was soft for a big man. He stared into the distance as we both fell silent.

"First rig?" I asked.

"Yeah, first."

"How's it treating you?"

"Like shit, but just glad to be working." It had been a long while since I had heard of a local Indian wanting to work.

"Right on. It's good to have you out here." I didn't really know how good it was—all I knew was it was a very positive thing that he wasn't dragging me out of the truck and pounding my skull with the tool of death that hung over his shoulder.

He kicked the dust and rocks under my driver door and looked straight into me. "Thanks." He again stared off into the distance at the dark land, and questions began to register, but I knew better than to ask an Indian about his homeland. "Vann wants to know if he should be watching out for that fish top?"

"Not yet. Let him know I'm working on the numbers and will be up there shortly."

"Gotcha." I watched as he nodded and looked back at the moon that hung over the rolling hills of the plains of North Dakota. "So what do you think is going to happen when we get downhole?"

"It's just going to depend," I replied.

"Depend on what?"

"Variables."

"Like what, tool hand."

"Mainly if we can screw into that tool joint or not."

"What if we can't?" I was starting to feel as if I was answering questions from an oversized nephew and wondered if I was going to get anything done in the next half hour.

"It all depends on how it feels and the depth in which we tag. If it feels light and mushy, then we will try circulating whatever is on top of it out of the well, be it sand or such. If it's a hard stop, we will most likely be on iron downhole such as the tool joint we want to screw into. Make sense?"

He turned back to the land and my eye took note of a scar stretching across his jugular that moved with his skin as he spoke. "I see." He nodded and I gazed at the tissue of a memory that I was sure he didn't want to relive. "So how exactly do you figure out what needs to be done with a well when it's got a fish?"

I cocked my head toward him with a slight smile. "You want to be a fishing hand or what?"

His eyes turned toward me and dug into my soul as his voice indicated that I had offended him. "You think I couldn't be? You think you're that special? I graduated from the University of North Dakota. I got the smarts to do your job." I was surprised but not impressed by the education and chuckled at the confidence.

"Never said that, did I?"

"No, I suppose not. Forgive me. I guess dealing with Jeff and Vann lately has me on edge." He turned his head, and I noticed snow starting to fill the hood of his duck coat as he spoke. "I figure it is pretty simple in my book. If I spend most of my time on a freezing cold rig floor covered in oil and drilling mud, raping and pillaging the land that my fathers tried so hard to protect, I should be able to make a future in this field. After all, this is my land." He shook his head and chuckled as I smiled at the irony of his ambition.

"This is true."

He nodded at me, and I heard a whisper come from the scars of his existence as he turned and slapped his hood over his hard hat. The buildup of snow fell onto his shoulders and surely onto the flesh of his back. He paid no attention to it—didn't shake any of it off, just kept walking—didn't flinch at the chill of the snow. He just walked off, not even looking back at me.

CHAPTER 15

Zebb's Dodge pulled up beside mine as darkness was still covering the sky. The dashboard clock read three a.m. We lowered our windows, and he stuck his meaty head out toward me, showing his bloodshot eyes wrinkled and crinkled from a lack of rest. "What do you think about Jesus?" His question shocked me to my core. I looked back over at the clock, trying to gather my thoughts, wondering if I might be dreaming.

The last time Zebb mentioned Jesus, he was determined to make him out as a lying Jew, and a fad. "Why do you wanna know?" I could only imagine the jokes he had worked on since our last job.

"'Cause I keep having these damn dreams. Crazy dreams. I mean flipping strange dreams." I wondered why he trusted me enough to tell me this and if he actually was curious or if he just didn't have anyone else to screw with at three in the morning.

"Like what?"

"I will tell you, but don't laugh."

"All right, I won't laugh. Just spit it out."

His pony tail fell out of his window onto the side of his truck as he spilled his revelation. "All right, every time I start getting good sleep a hand starts writing on a blackboard and spells out J-E-S-U-S. Each letter is written out slowly and methodically in old English letters in chalk like school teachers used to do."

"A hand?"

"Yes, a gosh-darn hand. I don't get it, and I can't

shake it." His frustration poured out, and confusion was etched across his face. I couldn't help and wondered why he would trust me with this information. I wondered if this was a set-up. If we dug into my faith, would he make a joke out of me? I had to take the risk, though.

"All right, Zebb, let's think about it. Does the hand ever write anything else?"

"No, just J-E-S-U-S! That's it. It writes it over and over and over just like when teachers used to make us do when you got in trouble."

"Do you think you are in trouble for something?"

"Not that I know of. I haven't done a fucking thing!" He paused for a moment and did a mental recall of the last 60 years. "At least that I know of. Nothing big anyhow." We both struggled with our thoughts as we looked over at the rig burying pipe in the earth stand after stand. We had less than three hours to tag the fish and to try and get screwed in, but I felt the countdown for his soul was more important.

"Zebb, we are all guilty of sin. It's just a matter of realizing it."

I watched as he rubbed his forehead in frustration "I don't get it. I just want to go to sleep, but I keep getting woke up by this Jesus feller, or his name, or whatever the hell is going on. I literally just want to sleep, but I can't! I don't care about sin or this Jesus!"

"Have you tried doing some homework on the whole dream thing or Jesus?"

"I'm not reading no fucking book on dreams. That's all bullshit. Them guys will tell you anything. I could write a book on that stuff—it's just opinions."

I reached on my dash for my Bible with a drilling rig

on the front cover from the Oilfield Christian Fellowship Ministry that had been given to me by a 35-year veteran of these oilfields. I looked at it, worn on the edges with a crinkle in the cover from my reading, then at Zebb, and handed it to him. "This book won't give you opinions, just facts and will tell you everything you want to know about J-E-S-U-S and your dreams."

"Let me see it." He shifted his weight toward my window, reached out for the book, and took it as I released my hold, delighted to give such a good book to a soul searching friend.

He thumbed through it. "Is this a Bible?"

"Yes, it's the New Living Translation. It's got some personal stories in there from other oil men who have asked the same thing."

"Did any of them have dreams?"

"Not that I know of, but there are several stories of answered dreams and interpretations of dreams throughout it."

"I'll take a look at it." He sat there momentarily flipping through pages and seemed lost in his own thoughts. "You never did tell me what you thought about Jesus?"

I thought of what my answer should be and on the fact that I had never actually had someone so bluntly ask me about Jesus. There were tons of things I could say about him. I could go into the history, the facts, the truth, the relationship He offers. I fought for an answer that would satisfy, but all I could say is what I felt deep within me. "Son of God, without a doubt. I believe he lived, and I believe he died and rose on the third day for our sins. He's my friend, my big brother, and the keeper of my heart. He has been known to be called the hound of heaven, and I believe that is just exactly what's behind your dreams." I felt a loving fierceness come from the pit of my stomach laced with the kindness of a heart tendered to someone actually curious about the Son of God. I wondered if my answer had been too straightforward, but I didn't know how else to answer. It was all I had.

His head cocked slightly in confusion. "What do you mean 'hound of heaven'?"

I paused for a moment to think of an explanation. "It means that like a hound, He will pursue the hunt at all costs once He gets onto your scent until He finds you. It's the same with Jesus. The only difference is that instead of a hound, you have a loving God who is hot on your trail, and all I can do is wish you luck on running or give you this Bible in hopes that you invite your Savior to walk alongside you every step of the way."

"So you think He is hot on my trail?"

"From what you've told me, I think your trail is on fire and something in you rejects it, runs from it, 'cause you know the hound is getting in close. Too close."

He looked at me thoughtfully. "What will happen if He catches me?"

I could only think of the time when the hound tracked me down and respond with that. "It will be a loving and wild ride my friend—anything could happen."

"I don't know about all that, but I appreciate your advice, and I will take a look at the book, but I'm going to head back and try to get some shut eye." He paused, sat the book on his dash, and turned back to me. "I would really appreciate you not saying anything about our conversation. Let's just keep it between us, you know."

"Not a problem." With that, he headed back over to his spot by the shacks and backed in for some much needed rest, hopefully. My heart felt for him—not pity, just anguish. I felt his pain not just for the lack of sleep but for his tormented soul. I could sense something pressing on him. My thoughts nagged at me. Who did I think I was to speak of the name of Jesus? I was so far from living right—the border of hypocrisy started to seep in. Was this really who I was? I couldn't give up drinking if I tried, couldn't stop cussing if my life depended on it, but I carried the name of Jesus on the same tongue. I shook away the negative thoughts. The fact was that I had come a long way since knowing Christ. Why should I hide that 'cause my lips still touched the bottle and spouted language inappropriate for a pulpit? I could reason with myself all day, but they all felt like excuses. The only thing I could do was follow what was buried in the deepest hollows of my heart.

I glanced back toward the 100-foot derrick sending pipe into the core of our molested planet. I double-checked my tired thoughts and hoped that Vann remembered to hold off before tagging the fish. I'm sure he did. He didn't strike me as a driller who lost track of things, but I figured I would make my way up and, if nothing else, have a cup of coffee and gather my bearings while Zebb hopefully rested.

The flakes were growing in heft as they stacked onto the hood of my Dodge. My ambition seemed to follow the snow—falling and stacking up. Molasses seemed to swirl in my head as I felt the pangs from a lack of sleep. It came with the territory—you just had to push through it once again as you counted the years it took off your life. I reached back and grabbed my jacket and grasped my tally book and stepped out and felt the flurries fall on the back of my neck. They melted, and I only hoped the wind would stay calm. I pushed my hard hat firmly onto my skull. My Redwing soles pounded the grated steel of the first step up to the rig floor, and my mind switched to what we had come here for—business, straight business. It was time to go to work. I knew it as I climbed the stairs and covered my hands with a new set of gloves. My soles pounded every steel step, my knees flexing as if I had entered an Olympic stair-stepping contest. Once at the top, I caught Vann's eye. I made my way to the driller stand as his palm leveled the brake, bringing the top drive to a stop, the thud jarring my bones as multiple tons of iron halted in the slips.

I confirmed with Vann that we were to start slowing down to keep us away from the Top of Fish (TOF) at 8870, something we did not want to run into due to the chance of damaging the top of the fish, making it very hard to catch.

I watched as the crew made up connection after connection, and the chalked numbers counted up as each stand swung out of the derrick. Ten to go, just enough time to grab a coffee. I headed inside the doghouse to check on the coffee pot. I could use the boost. Caffeine was my poison, and it usually did the trick on an early morning like this. The pot sat full of liquid gold. I could only assume that there was another addict around. Whether it was Vann or not was still to be determined, but the coffee was fresh. As the aroma hit my nostrils and started its work, I appreciated the sensation of feeling more alive. I prepared to screw into this fish and get it over with. My ears caught the familiar clack of elevators being slapped together, indicating Stand Eighty-One had just been latched. I poured the Styrofoam cup full while pondering over scenarios for latching onto this fish. As I bent the cup to my lips, I wondered if I would be able to screw into this fish easily or if it would fight me beyond my means. I wondered about the odds of junk or sand surrounding the threads downhole or casing collapsed on top of the connection. I gathered a contingency plan in my mind and shook off the concern.

I watched from the door of the doghouse as Vann buried stand after stand of drill pipe. A stand of drill pipe swung out, with Dakotah controlling it with his meaty, gloved hands, as he guided it to the connection awaiting.

I made my way beside Vann as he leveled the stand. "Whatta you think?" He asked.

"I think we are going to screw into this puppy and get to jarring."

"You think you will get her?"

I glanced at him and smirked. "Does a bear shit in the woods?" He grinned back at me. As I stood closely behind him, I prepped my mind for the worst but hoped for the best. He was no fool. He knew we were in a tight spot, and if things didn't play out for us the way we wanted, we would be in a much tighter spot. My mind reflected on the fact that if we took another kick, it might be our last. I quickly pushed the thought away.

I heard the clack elevators slapping shut from up above and felt the anticipation of getting close to the business end of this fish.

I spoke softly behind Vann. "Ease her on down very easy, and we will work with what she gives us." Vann nodded, sinking the stand of drill pipe deeper into the earth. I switched my gaze to the indicator, measuring every ton of pipe we were burying, a total of 90,000 pounds. "Vann, let's hold off here and get an up weight before we get too far ahead of ourselves." He nodded and flipped the rig's transmission into gear for pulling as his hand let up from the steel brake handle. He brought up the stand until the needle kicked over at 120,000. "Let's hold it there and get a neutral weight." I watched as the pipe steadied and the indicator followed, settling right above the usual 115k mark. "Looking good, looking good. Let's come on down and get screwed into this fish." The indicator followed the pipe down, giving us the feel of every curvature in the well as the needle jumped back and forth between 88 and 92. Most people believe that a vertical well is actually vertical. It's amazing the bends you can have when trying to drill 9,000 feet straight downhole. "You ready, Vann?"

He looked back at me with a sideways grin. "Does a bear shit in the woods and wipe his ass with a white rabbit?"

"Any day of the week."

"Well, there's your answer." I returned the grin and felt the steam of coffee brush my nose as I cherished the humor of a good driller.

We were approximately 90 feet off of the fish, and my blood started to percolate with excitement until I looked over the handrails of the floor as Vann went to dialing in his controls. I noticed Zebb on his way up, with Rikki not trailing far behind. Part of me hoped they wouldn't come up, but I knew they would. Something in old man Zebb always brought him up. He was known for being fast asleep, but as soon as something was about to happen, he was the first one up, Johnny on the spot—up without a doubt in boots, hat, and gloves. I took a sip of joe as Zebb made his way onto the rig floor, sticking out his meaty paw, which I firmly shook. He looked around, gathering his bearings as he glanced at the indicator and gauges. "Right on. How far out are you?"

"Sitting ninety feet away from fish top, just about

ready to screw into her."

Rikki came onto the floor shortly behind Zebb and seemed quiet, especially for the morning. I was grateful for it but wondered if it could last.

Zebb spoke as we waited for Vann to adjust controls. "You can head on out if you want." I glared at Zebb and glanced at my watch.

"It's only five forty-five. Change out is six."

Zebb returned a salty smile, knowing I wasn't leaving until we screwed into this fish together. Old Zebb was famous for glory stealing on these big jobs, coming up in the nick of time just to screw into a fish or get one out of the hole. I watched as Vann lowered the stand burying drill pipe, bringing us closer with every foot. We watched with anticipation, but then the back of my ears burned up as I heard Rikki speak up.

"Wait, Wait, Wait! We need to get on the same fucking page before we do this." I looked over in confusion at Rikki; Vann's squinted eyes reflected frustration as he forced the handle down, stopped the rig, and chained the brake.

"Well, let's go to the fucking dog house and talk then!" Vann spat out. I could barely suppress a laugh.

Rikki glared back toward Vann with demon spit flowing from his lips. "Don't speak to me like that, boy. I will run your ass off of location!"

"Well, we are either gonna talk about it or we gonna do it, one or the other. It can't be both. I'm just ready to get this son of a bitch outta the hole," Vann replied.

Rikki was already a ball of frustration; for someone to piss him off just a tad bit more was slightly entertaining.

"Let's go flipping talk about it, then," Vann said. We all headed toward the doghouse in a single-file line, like we were in grade school all over again. I felt the same frustration as Vann and thought of how many times we had gone over this with Rikki. What else could he possibly want to know? Did he want me to predict the future again, tell him that his well was shit, and tell him exactly what every scenario could possibly be? Maybe I should finally let the cat out of the bag and tell him I forgot my downhole goggles at the house.

We gathered in a circle with our feet planted on the white, painted steel floor. Rikki spoke with an arrogance that revealed his ignorance. "I just want you to know that this is my fucking well, and anything and everything that is to go on is to go on through me. Is that clear?" I quietly wondered how long it would take before I was run off. I wondered what it would be that I would do or wouldn't do. With a guy like Rikki, it was probably only a matter of time. Part of me just wanted to get it over with—run me off, run somebody off instead of this whole pins and needles thing. We all just stood there not saying a word in our circle as Rikki glared at each of our vacant, dreary faces.

His fist pounded the steel cabinet we knew to be the knowledge box and barked his orders. "We are not leaving this doghouse until we reach some kind of agreement. This is my fucking well! It's real simple, and if you don't like it, you can go to the house!" I wondered if Zebb and Vann thought, like I did, of volunteering to do just that.

Vann nodded his head in agreement, though, and Zebb nodded along, and I followed suit with a slight nod.

Rikki glanced back at me. "All right, what are we gonna do here then? Break it down for me, Wyatt."

I made rotations with my index finger into my palm as I started to speak. "We are simply going to come down and tag the fish top and put some slight rotation in and try to screw into her."

"Whatta you going to do if that doesn't work?"

"Just depends on what happens."

"What do you expect to happen?"

"There's no telling, Rikki. That fish could kick sideways, fall farther, have sand on top of it, get cross-threaded on us—there is really no telling until we get down there and give her what we got."

He glared at me, then quickly switched his stare to Zebb. "What are you going to do then, Zebb, since Wyatt doesn't seem to have a clue?"

Zebb put his index finger on his chin as his thumb cupped underneath in a perfect pose of an ancient Roman scholar. "Um, let me think on it."

"What the hell is that supposed to mean?"

"Hold on, I'm thinking."

"You have got to be fucking kidding me."

"Wait, wait, I think I got it. Yep, definitely got it. Whatever Wyatt wants to do sounds good to me." My heart filled with laughter, and I could hardly hold it in as Rikki's face grew beet red in frustration.

"Get the hell outta here and do your fucking job!"

"Yes sir," Zebb retorted as we bolted out the door without giving him a chance to rethink it and made a beeline back to the driller stand. Vann unchained the brake as I took my place behind him, waiting for him to switch into gear. He flipped the switch and looked back at me. "Whatta you wanna do, boss?"

"Come on down easy and let's tag her."

"Will do." His hand guided the steel of the brake

handle, letting it float as the top drive brought the string lower. I watched the needle of our indicator bounce between 85 and 91 and waited. I watched the drill pipe transfer through the floor, bringing us lower, and then I felt my feet twitch from a vibration familiar to any oilman.

Vann acted and stopped movement before I could blurt out the order. The needle barely twitched downward, but the feel in my feet told me more than any indicator. My feet were trained for this. We were right on top of the fish. I could only imagine the female part of drill pipe looking up at us. Was she kicked to the side? Were her threads damaged or filled with junk? I slowed down and took my time because it's easy to overthink this stuff. Zebb and Rikki stood several feet behind, watching, and, surprisingly, not crawling all over us, which was inherently nice. "Come on back up and give us a little rotation." Vann brought the pipe up a couple of feet and pushed a couple of buttons as I glanced at the torque. "Vann, let's go ahead and set your torque."

"Will do." Vann dialed in numbers on his screen, limiting us from damaging any connections on the packer.

"Bring her on down and let's see what we got." Vann switched gears and let off the brake, allowing the top drive to follow while inversely bringing down pipe slowly. I watched the needle twitch downward toward 87 as torque started spiking and slowing our rotations. "Come on up." Vann switched into gear and brought the pipe up, freeing up the torque and steadily rotating freely. "Come on back down and let's give her another try." I felt the vibration in my feet as we touched down on the fish with the same results. The torque spiked, stopping our rotation.

Vann looked back at me. "What now?"

"Come on back up and kick your pumps on about two barrels a minute." I waited and watched as Vann dialed his pumps in and got the derrick hand on the line to double-check valves. I caught Rikki out of the corner of my eye walking up around my side.

"Whatta you gonna do now?" he asked.

"Going to get these pumps kicked in."

"What you think that's going to help? You still going to have to screw into her."

"Yeah, I realize that, but it will help flush things out if there is junk in the threads, plus it will straighten and line things up downhole."

"Whatta you mean it lines stuff up?" Rikki asked. I started to wonder if this guy had ever done anything downhole or if he was just playing dumb. My expression must have revealed my thoughts as I cocked my head in surprise toward him. "Don't look at me like that. I wanna know what the hell you're doing down there before you fuck up my well."

"Think about it, Rikki. When you get all the pump pressure around drill pipe, it will make it stand up straighter."

"That's a bunch of bullshit."

"You think so, go ask Zebb and see what he thinks."

Rikki looked at his feet and seemed to think on his options. "Just get screwed in. I don't give a shit how you do it." He turned his back and walked away.

Vann nodded back toward me. "We're ready." I glanced up at the newly installed Kelly hose kicking, indicating we were indeed pumping downhole. "What? You don't trust me?"

I returned his smirk. "Just an old habit, I guess." I always liked to see some kind of proof of things going on, I suppose. "All right, let's get her. Bring it on down, Mr. Trustworthy." He laughed and kicked the rotation in and started down slowly. We tagged the fish. I started to see a torque spike bouncing around, and I sensed hesitation from Vann. "Set it down just a touch more." Vann let up on the brake, bringing drill pipe down only a couple inches and spiking our torque. I quickly responded, "Bring her on up." I watched in anticipation as Vann switched over and brought the drill pipe up. I watched the weight indicator needle spike and kick over freely at 90K.

"Whatta you wanna do, boss?"

"Hold her right there." I sensed we were starting to successfully screw into our connection downhole. I clocked seven seconds and watched the torque start to kick upwards. "Bring her on up and keep that rotation going." He lifted off the brake as drill pipe rose up. If I was right, we would pull over and torque up, indicating we were connected.

Vann asked, "How high you wanna bring her?"

"Bring her up to our up weight of one-thirty-five K." We torqued up, and he pulled the drill pipe upwards, with the needle of the weight indicator following.

He nodded toward to the indicator and looked back at me. "That's one-thirty-five. You think we got her?"

"Does a bear shit in the woods?" His head cocked back in a laugh that echoed around me. The job might be hell, but Vann was good company.

"You that certain, huh?"

"Certain enough that I would wipe my own ass with a white rabbit if it's not."

"I'm holding you to that."

I laughed and then retorted, "As long as you don't

hold it on me."

"It's all yours, big man." I smiled at Zebb and slapped my tally book into his palm. He returned the smile and slapped me on the back.

"See you at six o'clock."

"Yeah, see you at six." I turned and headed off the floor, but my curiosity kicked in before I descended the first stair, and I turned back to Zebb. "You going to jar most of the day or what's your plan?"

"Plan is to give her hell all day, jar all day if we have to, try to release that packer if she lets us, wash her up when I feel like it. We'll just see what she gives us. Whatever it is, we'll take it. That's the plan, little buddy." He gave me a wink.

I dismissed any other thoughts and left the burden of thought upon his shoulders. It was called relief for a reason. It was time to get out of here. I took each stair with a sense of freedom and headed down to my truck. I threw my hard hat in the back and loaded myself inside. I couldn't remember how long I had been up. It didn't matter; it was all part of it, part of the life. I gazed at the digits on my dash; it read 6:11 a.m.

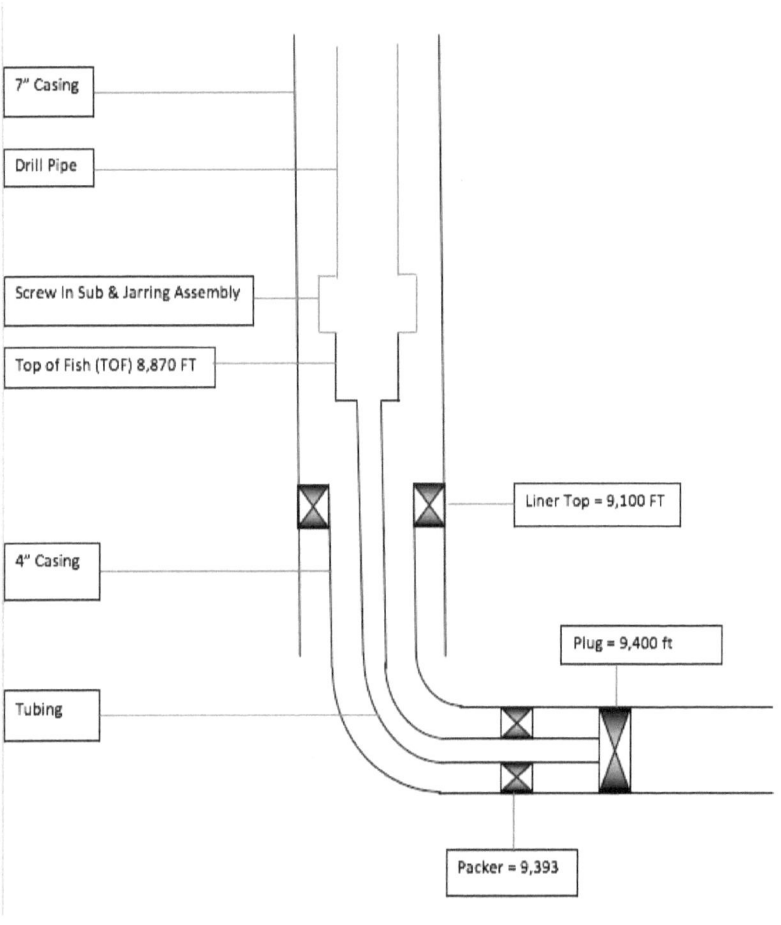

7" Casing

Drill Pipe

Screw In Sub & Jarring Assembly

Top of Fish (TOF) 8,870 FT

Liner Top = 9,100 FT

4" Casing

Plug = 9,400 ft

Tubing

Packer = 9,393

CHAPTER 16

I chugged into the parking lot of the Airport International Inn for my destiny with sleep. I felt drugged, lethargic, as my body lumbered out of the truck. The soles of my Redwings sank through the snow beneath them as I stepped to the side door of the hotel and swiped my entry card: a red "X" flashed. I made the long trek to the front desk across the dingy carpet that was stained with dirt and grime; a musty stench radiated off the flooring. An Asian woman sporting the standard hotel maroon, looking out of place in a North Dakota boomtown sat behind the front desk.

I neared the desk and tried to control my frustration. My mind felt like syrup was sloshing around inside it from the weariness and lack of sleep. I spoke with what I thought reflected a calm temperament. "My card doesn't work."

Her voice was pleasant as she brought archives up on the computer. "What room you are in, sir?"

"Four-fifty-nine."

"That room booked, sir."

"I know it's booked. I booked it."

"Room booked by someone else, sir."

My eyes widened in disbelief. "Excuse me?"

She replied with the emotion of a trained robot. "Yes, sir, that room booked." Behind her, on the floor, sat plastic trash bags crammed to the rim. The collar of a shirt peeking out of the top of one of them looking oddly familiar.

My tone of civility made a quick departure. "Is that all my shit behind you?" I felt regret as the words left my mouth but was too tired to care.

She stared at her computer without making eye contact as her mechanical tone replied. "Yes, we bagged it. It behind me."

"You did what?"

"We bag you clothes."

"I paid for two nights, two nights ago, with a check out time of eleven a.m. It's seven-thirty in the morning. Technically, I got the room for another three-and-a-half hours."

She looked up from her screen and flashed a slight smile that I wanted to wipe off her face. "You weren't in room, sir."

"Doesn't matter. I paid. Look lady, I'm not sure how they do things in Northwest Asia, but here in America, you generally get what you pay for."

"Sir, I sorry, but you no room."

"Have you got any other rooms since you apparently sold mine?"

She flashed her robotic smile once again. "Not at this time, sir, but you try back tomorrow."

"That really doesn't help me, lady. Just give my stuff, so I can leave this shithole." I heard the familiar clink of my Jack Daniel's bottle against my Mason jar as she dragged my bags around to the side of the desk, went and sat back down, and without even an apologetic glance my way, became absorbed again in her computer.

I threw one bag over my shoulder and dragged the other one along the grungy carpet. The bottle of Jack clanking ominously around in the bag. Halfway to the door, I heard a loud commotion coming from the desk behind me. Some man was screaming violently at Miss Asia about a room. From what I could make out, it sounded like opportunity. I turned on my heels, dragging my bags back behind me, and wandered back to the desk in order to hear the commotion. I noticed an imitation of a white Fat Albert dressed in oilfield clothing pacing back and forth, yelling at Asia. He stammered and put his index finger to her face and yelled viciously, "GIVE ME BACK MY MONEY!"

I saw her shivering in fear, standing meekly with her arms by her side and a tear working its way down her cheek. Strange, maybe, but I felt no vindication seeing her that way.

I kept a safe distance behind Fat Albert and dared to speak up. "What's going on, man? Maybe I can help."

He turned and eyeballed me. "Not unless you want to pay me for my fucking room," he spat out. "If not, then I suppose you had better get lost." His words weren't an idle threat. He looked like he ate something the size of me for breakfast. I wondered if maybe I had just spoken my last words. My mind clicked to the half-empty bottle of Jack Daniel's that might even things up a bit if I could get to it quick enough and score a shot over his skull if the situation escalated.

"You may just be in luck. If you got a room for the afternoon, I'll pay you for it."

He glared back at me. "How much?"

"Whatever the going rate is." I looked past Fat Albert's broad shoulders to make eye contact with Asia. "What's the rate, ma'am?"

"Two hundred and fourteen dollars." I pulled my wallet out, took out some traveling cash, and counted out two hundred dollar bills and a twenty.

His tempered alleviated once the money hit his hand. He spoke up. "I'm sorry about my behavior, but I—"

I waved my hand to interrupt him. "—really don't wanna hear it. You can apologize to her if you feel bad about it, but for me, just give me your keycard." I held my hand out and he slapped the card in my hand and turned to Asia and nodded as he picked up his luggage and left the building. I glanced at the keycard for Room 230 and turned to walk to my newfound room.

A small voice came from behind the counter. "Thank you."

I turned back to her and nodded. "You're welcome." I wondered if this was her first oil town to work in. My guess was that it probably was.

I dragged my bags and ragged body to Room 230, slid the keycard through, a beautiful green light flashed, and I opened the door to a room that apparently even for $220 didn't get cleaned but once a week. I couldn't believe I had just paid over two hundred dollars for this dirty old room. The civilized side of me was disgusted as I walked past dirty towels lying on the tiled floor of an even filthier bathroom floor with the grout stained dark brown from years of lack of cleaning.

I took a seat at the desk, eased off my boots, and took the time to unpack my trash bags and set the bottle of Jack on the desk. I pulled out the Mason jar and sniffed it—as if something would have changed since yesterday. It still held the stench of dried-up Jack and coke. I thought about cleaning it, but as I poured the dark liquor into the jar, I preached to myself about the sanitizing properties of Jack Daniel's. The liquor poured as I pondered Zebb's question about the name of Jesus on the wall, and I thought about the theological ramifications of sipping Jack while thinking about Christ. But, as I took a sip and felt my blood start to thin and my nerves ease, I pushed those sentiments aside.

I kicked my feet up on the desk, and I wondered how long Zebb had been having dreams. I pondered why I had never had those kinds of dreams. Maybe Jesus figured that wasn't the best way to get through to me. Everybody knows He works in mysterious ways. I also wondered if what I had said to Zebb had helped him or hurt him. His situation caused me deep concern, and I deeply hoped that I had helped. *Just maybe*, I thought, *he might read the Bible I had handed to him.* I knew we probably wouldn't talk much more about the subject due to the weight of it. I hoped in that brief moment of exposure that I had done right by him.

I nursed the drink as my thoughts switched to the job. I hoped that Zebb would have some kind of luck jarring. I wondered how long Rikki would allow him to jar before shutting him down. That Rikki, he was something else. I just couldn't get a read on the guy. I bet he was a totally different cat off the rig. I took another sip, and my mind drifted to Jessica. Red digits reading 8:45 a.m. radiated off the nightstand clock. She was an hour behind me in Dillon, and I wondered if she was up. I was sure she was—she seemed like an ambitious lady. I wondered if she felt like talking—it would be nice to hear her sweet voice—but I was too tired to talk and didn't want to talk while falling off to sleep, even though she likely wouldn't mind. I couldn't help speculating on what it would feel like to lie next to her. I took one more sip, pondered her kiss, shot back the remainder of poison, and slipped in between the sheets.

. . . .

I rolled over and glanced at my phone. It read 3:13 p.m. and flashed that three new voicemails and a text that had come through. All three calls were from Zebb's number—this could not be good. I held the voicemail button firmly down as my head rested against the cheap wooden headboard. Zebb's voice rumbled over the line and told me to get my ass out of bed and into the shop to pick up tools ASAP. I looked back at the call log: time of call read 1:19 pm. It wasn't the way I wanted my day to start, but it was the nature of the beast, and if that old fart couldn't be here to drag me out of bed, he would use an extension. Every one of his messages said the same thing: *Get the hell out here, I need some tools!*

I deleted his messages, glanced at the phone one more time and swung my feet off the mattress. My feet hit the floor; I felt a crunch beneath me. I lifted my foot and looked. A saltine clung to the ball of my foot, and its crumpled grains filled the gaps in my toes. *Disgusting!* I purged my toes clean and wiped the cracker from the bottom of my feet. Where in the hell did that come from? Unfortunately, I had no time to ponder the mystery of the murdered saltine. I gathered my socks, dug out a pair of oil-stained coveralls that had been buried deep in the packed Hefty, and made my way outside. As the chill met me, I brushed my cheeks and snow found the back of my neck. I trekked my way to my truck, with each step sinking in the fluff of snow leaving over a five-inch deep imprint.

. . . .

My tires edged onto the gravel of our tool shop lot as I backed the Dodge up to an open bay door and stepped out, letting the wind chill my bones. I hurried my way into the office and climbed the stairs to find Bryant standing and staring at the same white board we had reviewed a couple of days ago. "How's it going?" I asked. It startled him out of his trance.

"Hey there, stranger. Zebb's being trying to get ahold of you."

"Yeah, I realized that as soon as I rolled over."

"Well, you're here now. You aware of current status?"

Curiosity coursed through my bones. "No, I'm not. What's going on?"

"Zebb jarred all day except for the times pressure was trying to kill him." Bryant sat down behind his desk and leaned back, clasping his hands behind his head.

"Any luck?" I asked

"Well, he's still alive. I would say that's as good as it gets."

"That bad?"

He leaned forward, looked me dead in the eye, and tapped his index finger down on his hardwood desk. "We are getting our asses kicked out there. There's nothing you guys have done wrong, but it doesn't matter. The blame is coming down the pipe, and they are talking about running us off location."

My reply rang out in disbelief. "What! You gotta be kidding me."

"Yeah. It is what it is, though. We just gotta change some things up."

"What you got in mind?"

"I'm thinking 'washover.'"

"You sure you wanna go down that road?"

"Not a matter of whether I want to or not. I think we have to."

"You do remember we will be horizontal, and that would put our washpipe out close to ninety degrees. We side load it, we are done with a capital D."

"Yes, I know. The fact is, they want to see something happen instead of jarring all week."

"Oh, they're gonna get something happening, all right."

"C'mon, man. We've milled out sideways a thousand times."

"Yeah, but hundreds of feet of washpipe have also been left down hole from doing it."

"This is true, but we really don't have a choice here. Sometimes you just got to start changing things up and go for it."

"All right, you're the boss. Let's go for it." I walked downstairs and eyed the tools that awaited me.

I glanced down at a three-foot shoe that was as round as my head and as thin as a soda pop can, at least by oilfield standards. I ran my fingers against the rugged carbide on the bottom. I measured her up, down, and center and double-checked the numbers against the measurements of the casing it was going into. This would be what would go over the stuck packer and drill around it, clearing up any obstruction.

"Look good?" It was a question from Harry Clark, our welder. Most shops don't realize the value of a good welder, but one can make or break a shop in a moment's notice, and Harry was one of the best. Salty, with about 20 years on me and sporting the effects of thousands of Budweisers around his waist that probably would never work themselves off, Harry was a good fellow who had built me tools before when I had been up here in North Dakota doing some jobs.

"Yep, looks good," I replied

"I was talking it over with Bryant, and he said this would be the kind of shoe you would want. Just wanted to make sure before it got sent out to you. Sounds like you guys got a hell of job out there."

"That's one way to put it. I think the shoe will do us just fine. Thanks." I shook his hand for good measure, threw the shoe in the back of the truck along with a couple of crossovers, and jumped into the Dodge.

. . . .

I glanced at the green digits radiating from the dashboard clock that read 5:30 p.m. I rounded thirteen-mile corner headed toward Tioga and bound for location. My thoughts rambled like the tools doing the same on the steel of the truck bed.

Nothing on the radio struck my interest. My thoughts drifted to Jessica, and the thought of calling her suddenly seemed quite appealing. I punched the call button beside her name and after a second ring, I heard the sweetness of her voice radiate through the line.

"Hey, there." The softness in her voice warmed my soul. She seemed to genuinely want to talk.

"What are you up to?" I asked.

"Just on break from class, trying to catch some fresh air outside. Pretty stuffy inside."

"I see. So, how's it going?" I cheerfully asked, not really sure what to say or where to take the conversation, a normal dilemma, I figured for such a green relationship as ours.

I heard a touch of excitement in her voice. "Pretty good."

"Yeah, how so?"

"I found out today that I got into the A-I class I've been applying to for a year!" Her voice rang with genuine excitement, which caused me to be excited for her even though I had no idea what to be excited about. What the hell was an AI class?

"That's good! When does it start?"

"Next week. It's a three-day course, Friday through Sunday. They were able to fit me in last minute."

"That's exciting! Where's the class at?"

"It will actually be right there in Williston."

"Really? So, I will be seeing you soon?"

"Yep, if you can bear it."

"I'll have to grit my teeth, but I think I can bear it."

She laughed, and I was thankful she spoke sarcasm. "I'm looking forward to it. Maybe you will be off that job by then," she replied.

"I doubt it, but I'm sure I can work something out."

"I'm pretty excited. I've been looking forward to this class for a long time and have been putting the money back for it. They are very selective, so I'm happy about it."

"I'm happy for you. What exactly will you be doing?"

"Artificial insemination. Impregnating cows and such."

"Gotcha."

"It will help with what I want to do for ranches."

"That's good. So where are you going to stay while you're in Williston?"

"I was thinking of staying at the Airport International Inn. They seem to have good reviews online."

"They must be writing their own."

"Is it not so good?"

"That's an understatement." My mind went back to the hooker next door and Fat Albert. "Just take it from me, you don't want to stay there. Don't do that to yourself."

"Is it that bad?"

"Let's just say that I have been staying there, and it's not worth the two hundred and fourteen dollars a night."

"Two hundred and fourteen dollars a night! That's what I pay a month in Dillon!" I could hear the panic in her voice. "I can't pay that."

"Yeah, it's pretty steep. But, hey, I got a friend that might let you stay at his place. His wife would probably enjoy the company."

"They pretty good people?"

"Exceptional. Known them for years."

"You don't think they would mind?"

"Don't think so. It's only for a weekend; they got plenty of extra rooms."

"I just don't want to intrude."

"It's either that or you sleep in your car in a town that's eighty percent male with rape starting to become the norm." I wasn't trying to convince her; I genuinely wanted her to be safe and I hoped she realized that.

"I could pay them."

"They wouldn't accept it. Cady could use the company. Women don't really get to get out much around here just 'cause of all the mess that's going on."

"Who is Cady?"

"Bryant, my boss, his wife."

"All right, let's plan on it then, as long as they are okay with me staying there."

"Sounds like a plan. I'll let you know if they aren't."

She changed topics. "By the way, how's that job going?"

I wanted to reply "like dog shit," but figured it probably wasn't the best response to a lady, so I said the second best thing on my mind. "Like shit." There was just no other way to describe it without sugar coating it. I immediately regretted my language. I knew I had fallen back into oilfield dialect, all too quickly.

"Oh." She sounded concerned. "I'm sorry to hear that."

"Yeah, if we weren't fighting pressure that keeps acting very much out of the ordinary, it wouldn't be too bad, but we are leaning toward the fact that the pressure has now possibly collapsed casing onto my tools."

"So you don't actually know what's going on down there?"

"To be honest, nobody ever knows exactly what's going on down there. Anyone that says they do is a liar. There are so many variables being almost 10,000 feet down hole, you go off of previous experiences and your best guess from the indications you get and your gut."

"I see. I guess I thought there were definitive ways you went about things."

"It's hard to explain. There is and there isn't. Does that make any sense?"

"Not really, but you can explain it more later. It sounds very neat though, and like you get to deal with something different every day."

"Yeah, that's very true, which I think is good for me. I just wouldn't do very well in a nine-to-five, sit-at-your-desk job. This oilfield stuff definitely keeps your mind going. There is always another problem to figure out."

"That's interesting. I guess I didn't realize it was that involved. I'm not foolish enough to believe that you just stick a straw in the ground and oil comes shooting out, but I guess I never really thought of how much actually goes into it."

"There's actually quite a bit that goes along with this business. If you don't like problems, then you probably shouldn't be in the oil business."

"I see. Well, I should probably get my bum back in class."

"Yeah, probably so. It was good talking to you, though," I said.

"Yes. Very good." The kindness of her voice warmed me. She conveyed pure honesty and genuine concern, holding nothing back, traits you can't come across often enough.

I felt a smile break across my cheeks. "Talk to you later?"

"Definitely so. Goodbye." With that we hung up, and I wondered what it would be like to say "I love you" to her. Not now, it was way too soon, but maybe someday. What did it take to get to that level? I guess you just gotta feel that burn in your soul of not wanting anyone else, that burn of not wanting to spend one more moment without her, without her voice, without her hand holding yours, without her love. I think that's the time when you say it.

I returned my concentration to the road and focused my mind back on the job—on the thought of pressure starting to come back at us and getting this fish out. My tires slung up gravel as I left the asphalt, passing county road signs and rounding a corner as I zipped the Dodge past a working frack job with steam and smoke rolling off of a dozen or so trucks. My eyes caught sight of our rig in the distance. I eyed the derrick and tried to spot a black leg of drill pipe indicating they were out of the hole, but no such luck. I pulled onto location, backed up beside Zebb's empty truck, and stepped out to face the cold. The snow met me point blank in the face as I positioned my hard hat onto my skull and tightened the strap behind. My Redwings touched down on the first step leading up to whatever hell awaited me on the rig floor.

....

"Hey, you little fucker, I thought you'd never get here," Zebb said as I noticed his clothes soaked through in oil, strange for a supervisor, especially Zebb. I flashed a smirk and shook the meaty hand he thrusted toward me. It was his typical friendly oilfield hello, and I knew his knees had to be aching from standing all day on the iron floor. I knew all too well that on a good day of jarring, your relief couldn't get there quick enough. Vann stood beside Zebb and leaned away from the brake handle to give me a quick shake.

"Good morning," he said. I looked at the sun starting to set behind the hills and smiled at the irony of the statement.

"Good morning," I replied as Vann who had the privilege to stay over due to his relief getting run off for failing a random drug test leaned back onto the brake handle and Zebb continued his directives and I glanced around at the fresh oil that painted the derrick legs and rig floor.

I watched the needle on the weight indicator follow up as Vann brought the drill string up toward the sky, pulling fifty thousand pounds over, as we waited.

BAM! I felt the vibrations flow through my feet and up to my shoulders as the jars hit downhole, rattling the derrick and sending vibrations all the way up through our bones. I gave a slight jump at impact, startled by the ferocity of the jars, and felt an immediate elbow jab me in the side. I looked over at Zebb and Vann snickering. Zebb seemed to be trying to get a full laugh out but couldn't due to the Marlboro Man that lived in his lungs.

I shook it off with a smile and returned an elbow in his side. "Fuck you, Zebb." He only tried to laugh harder. I thought he might hack out a lung. I watched as his head bent over his belly. He was trying to catch his breath while still trying to laugh. "You going to make it?" I asked.

He rose up and shook it off, still faintly chuckling. "Yeah, but that's the funniest thing we've seen all day."

"Glad I can help you out with it." The first action of jarring threw me off, like the first shot being fired off at the range without muffs on. I knew the jar was coming, but subconsciously I wasn't ready for the hit.

"No movement," Zebb said and jotted a note in his tally book.

"Has it moved for you at all today?" I asked.

"Not a bit."

Zebb instructed Vann to lower the drill string and let the jars rest, giving us a convenient time to go downstairs and make relief at our trucks. When we got to the trucks, Zebb leaned into his cab to grab a handful of shop rags and a bottle of GO-JO and started cleaning the grime from his hands.

"What do you think?" I asked.

He continued to scrub and wipe the grease from his hands and replied with the professionalism you would expect from a multi-million dollar operation. "A three-hundred-pound dog is a big son of a bitch."

My head cocked to the side in perplexity. That was the second time I'd heard him utter the phrase. The statement was very true: a 300-pound dog was in fact a huge dog, and I did ask him what he was thinking, and, apparently, that was it. What do you say to it?

I smiled, knowing that I wasn't going to get much more than that out of him. It actually seemed like he didn't give a shit. "Give me your tally book and go get some sleep,"

"Wouldn't that be nice?" He retorted as he took less than a second to slap his worn-out leather tally book in the palm of my hand with the words "Gotta Feel It" inscribed on the front. I wondered exactly what that meant. I wondered if it meant the same to me as it did to him, but I really didn't want another 300-pound dog answer and figured it not worth asking.

I relayed the new instructions from Bryant. "I'm going to try and release that packer one more time, then I'm coming out of the hole to wash over it." I watched as he threw the greasy rags in the toolbox and climbed in the cab of the Ram.

I stood there as he settled in the driver's seat and leaned out the open window. "On a serious note, Wyatt, we are on the same page. I don't think this son of a bitch is going to be jarred out, not at this time. We got some messed-up shit going on downhole."

"What happened?"

"We were jarring and took a kick, a pretty bad one, and it came from nowhere. The pits started overflowing as drilling fluid came screaming over the shakers, and gas monitors for H_2S started going off, and we had to choke it out and circulate for hours. It was a son of a bitch. We had control but just barely. It wouldn't have taken much for us to lose the well."

"Damn it."

"Yeah, damn it is right. It was almost a pretty shitty deal. It's like this well is insane and can't decide whether or not to blow us up or let us have another chance to retrieve that fish."

"How did Rikki handle the whole thing?"

"He was off of location, probably screwing some whore or drinking beer for all I know. The guy is a fucking idiot. He said he was going to the office in town, but I doubt it."

"Did he ever come back?"

"Yeah, we ended up having a conference call with his engineer, and I told him that we needed a snubbing unit out here to deal with this pressure, and he basically told me to screw off, and they weren't going to spend that kind of money."

"You have got to be fucking kidding me."

"Nope, not a bit. The whole conversation, they pretty much ignored everything I had to say. The engineer spent most of the time telling Rikki what was going on. He was just clueless."

"Unbelievable."

"Yes indeed."

I stared down at my boots and thought about the gravity of working with an idiot like Rikki on this kind of well and the fact that we now were facing one of the most poisonous gases in the world, H2S- hydrogen sulfide, the same gas that was among the chemical compounds Hitler used in concentration camps to kill millions of Jews, it held the very distinctly smell of rotten eggs. We were talking about something that could burn this whole show to the ground. The reality that I might not make it home from this well hit me like a ton of bricks. Zebb was now all business, which probably burned more fear into me than anything. Zebb was never all business. It had been awhile since I had strapped on boots and thought about the sobering reality that I might not be coming home after my shift. I've had brothers in the field die due to this kind of kick, and Zebb's words hit home when he looked me dead in the eye with the seriousness of life and death on the table and spoke up. "Be careful. Don't let this bitch get the best of you." I solemnly nodded my head, knowing and trusting that if he was nervous, I had a right to be scared shitless. This really was starting to become a well from hell.

He leaned back inside the cab and dispensed some parting wisdom. "Be careful, buddy, knock 'em dead, and get this motherfucker out by the time I get back, so we can get the hell outta here and have a beer."

I wish I could say that my nerves eased, but they weren't—far from it. The technical side of a kick didn't concern me. I cut my teeth in high-pressure gas fields; we lived and breathed drilling underbalanced and gas kicks. I had experienced the uncertainty of a kick, even as a young roughneck. I had watched a sister rig burn to the ground when flames blew past the crown of the derrick. I remember the feeling of that day as I watched men run for their lives while fire burrowed through the rig, lighting up the dark night.

Nevertheless, I pushed my fears aside and felt my blood thicken with adrenaline. I knew it was time to go to work, and I felt the cold wind start to put a chill down the back of my neck that flowed through my spine. I reached behind and ratcheted my hardhat strap, feeling the clinch around my skull as I cranked on the ratchet to keep the wind from stealing a piece of armor from me.

CHAPTER 17

I stuffed Zebb's leather-bound tally book in my back pocket and looked up at the rig that awaited me; it was eerily quiet while the jars downhole were resting. I had to put my fears aside. If I entertained it, it would only affect my decisions. I was trained—highly trained but I knew there was a high possibility that I could be coming home in a body bag. Every choice had led up to this moment, jobs like this made or broke a good tool hand; there wouldn't be any war stories to tell if everybody turned away from battle.

My feet touched the first steel stair toward the iron rig floor as a prayer solemnly escaped my lips. "Lord, let my thoughts be quick, but my feet quicker, for You are in control, even 10,000 feet beneath the earth. Lord, You are in control. Protect me and let me return from my shift. Amen." I felt strengthened, and my steps grew confident; my Redwings hardly touched steel as I climbed my way to the top of the floor.

. . . .

I arrived on the rig floor and spied Vann leaning against the driller's stand, waiting on orders. "Boss, you wanna start back jarring or what?"

"Don't see what good it would do us. They jarred all day. Don't think it's going to change just because I got here."

"Aw, come on. You don't have that magic touch?"

"Can't say I do, at least not today."

"What do you want to do then, Mr. No Magic?"

"Going to try and release that packer."

"Really? You think she will release?"

"No, not really, but it's worth a shot."

"Boy, you're full of optimism today."

"Just wanna try my magic."

"Yeah, that's what I told her." I chuckled at his reply; it was grade school, but funny, nonetheless.

I motioned to Vann. "Come on down and let's see what we got." Vann lifted up on the brake handle, bringing the drill string down with weight stacking in the same place as when I left this morning. "Well, wasn't much change there, was it?"

"Not a bit."

"All right, come on down and set about 10 K down on that packer." I watched as the drill string buried deeper, and the needle ticked at 80K, letting 10,000 pounds rest on the fish.

"All right, put a half turn to the left and come on up." The drill pipe rotated from the power of the top drive. Vann switched the rig into gear and lifted up on the brake as the engines roared, and the draw works wrapped drill line around its spool, bringing the string of pipe up while transmitting a powerful force through the drill string to my screw-in sub and down to my packer that I had sent downhole only a couple days ago. The thought crossed my mind that perhaps something was wrong with my packer. It wasn't likely, but what if my tool had malfunctioned downhole? It was a possibility, just not one I wanted to think about.

I watched as the drill string came up pulling weight into the fish, and the needle followed, passing the 120K mark. I watched as the needle bobbled at 120.

Vann asked, "You see that bobble?"

"I did indeed. Keep on coming up." It was almost comical to make decisions on a slight bobble or a kick of a needle that would have gone unnoticed or ignored in many situations, but it was all we had to go on, and it indicated a free point in the pipe. When it's all you got, it's just that.

I stood watching, feeling a little disbelief that she was really coming free, but excited all at the same time. My soul surged as I thought about actually getting off this well sometime soon. Vann steadily inched the drill string up as we tried with limited options to wiggle the fish through any obstructions as slowly as possible. All the jarring and beating must have freed something up in order for us to be able to release the packer. I watched the indicator like a hawk watching prey as Vann maintained the handle, still easing up the drill string and moving our fish up the hole inch by inch. It was the moment we had strived so hard for.

The excitement ran deep as the needle maintained at 120K, and Vann looked over at me with the biggest grin I had seen out of him yet. "FUCK, YEAH! We got her, boss!" As soon as the words left his mouth, my feet felt a vibration that reverberated from downhole just as the needle climbed to 135K.

"Damn it, Vann, you had to say it, didn't you?"

He shook his head in aggravation and forcefully pushed the handle down, stopping any more overpull. "Yeah, I guess I did." The wiser part of both of us knew that his words didn't stop the hundred and twenty thousand pound drill string from moving, but it was a rule—you never say *you got it* until she is on the bank.

"Let's see if we can jar through this and bring it on up," I ordered. Vann nodded and turned back to the brake and lifted on the handle, bringing the drill string up and pulling against the fish. The needle climbed higher, passing 135K and moving like an iron rock to 145K, then 155K. "Hold her right there. Let those jars hit," I barked as we stood there waiting in anticipation.

Bam! I felt the jars hit and the derrick shake, rattling my bones, but not a bit of movement from the fish. We were stuck once again.

I walked over to the drill string, made a mark of where we had moved to, and measured.

I heard Vann holler from behind his stand. "Did we move her at all?"

I walked back to Vann, shaking my head in frustration. "A foot."

"Well, that's better than nothing."

"This is true."

I pulled Zebb's worn-out leathered tally book from my back pocket and jotted our movement.

"All right, come on down and see if we can cock those jars." Vann drove pipe through the floor and tried to stack weight on our assembly down hole.

"Got it!"

"Good, let's get to jarring then."

"Will do, boss."

"I'm gonna grab a cup of coffee."

"All right sounds good. Bring me one over, would you?"

"Will do." I turned and went inside the steel doghouse cabin and started pouring a cup of coffee as Vann brought the drill string up and pulled weight into the jars.

Bam!

I felt the vibrations go through me, barely even noticing as I sipped my coffee. The aroma filled my nostrils with every sip while I thought over the matter at hand as Vann continued jarring.

Bam!

I looked at the door of the doghouse and caught sight of Rikki starting to make his way up the stairs to the floor. I turned and made my way back to the coffee pot to pour me a refill and fill a cup for Vann.

I sat his cup above his controls. He nodded toward me, giving thanks as he maintained his stare on the indicator while bringing the drill string back up for another episode of jarring.

Bam!

Vann's cup of coffee jumped several inches into the air. He grabbed the cup mid-air as some of the black gold spilled over, soaking through his cotton gloves. He took a sip and nodded to me.

I nodded back and spoke up. "I think our luck just ran out," I said.

"I thought our luck ran out days ago."

"Rikki is on his way up here," I retorted.

"Yep, our luck has definitely run out, my friend." Vann clutched out and lifted the handle, letting the drill string fall back through the floor to cock the jars. "How long 'til he is up here?"

I looked at my watch, remembering how long it took him to climb. "About six minutes. He just left his shack."

"Gotcha. You wanna keep jarring?"

"Yeah. I'm assuming he will probably want to change some things up, but for now, let's keep jarring."

"All right." Vann switched the rig into gear and brought the drill string back up.

Bam!

No change. We jarred an additional eleven times, and I glanced at my watch and noticed a seven-minute time difference from when I had previously checked.

"Where you think he is?" Vann asked

"Hell if I know." I walked over to the stairs to see if we had any luck remaining as the moon hung over the hills, Rikki was halfway up but apparently needed a rest. I felt bad for him as I watched him engulf air, trying to catch his breath as he rested his weight on the handrails. He inhaled vigorously, glanced up and spotted me eyeing him, and quickly started up the stairs again. I turned away and went back to the driller's stand.

Bam!

"Is he coming up or what?"

"He's trying."

"What do you mean he's trying?"

"I mean he's out of breath and trying not to die about halfway up."

"You got to be fucking kidding me. Are you telling me Mr. Fatass can't even make it up the stairs?"

"Pretty much." Vann just shook his head in disgust and brought the drill string back down, cocked the jars, and immediately brought them back up.

Bam!

Rikki made his way onto the floor. I looked over to see him bent over and resting again before he made his way to us. Another tinge of sympathy for him washed over me.

Rikki approached us as Vann lowered the drill string.

"How's it going?"

I turned my head toward him. "Like shit."

"Looks like you moved it a little bit."

"Yeah, we were able to get the packer unset and move it up."

Rikki's arms flew up in the air "That's great! What do you mean '*like shit*'" he exclaimed.

"We're stuck again."

"That's all right. We'll get her." I watched as the drill string rose.

Bam!

I looked over at the needle of the weight indicator not budging and the mark on our pipe still sitting at the floor. "I hope so." He patted me on the back, which felt strangely unusual. "Let's give her another hour. You'll get her."

"I hope so," I replied as Rikki went into the doghouse, most likely in search of coffee.

"That was different," I said.

Vann gave me a smirking grin. "You couldn't smell his breath?"

"No." The second after I said it, the reeking stench of alcohol hit me along with the realization of where he had been during Zebb's shift.

CHAPTER 18

"Shut her down and leave it hanging with about fifty thousand pulled into it, and let's get some coffee." We had been jarring and beating on the packer for over an hour, trying without an ounce of luck every trick in the book to get things freed up. It was crazy, but I've gotten more fish out of the hole by patiently waiting and leaving a drill string pulled into tension then beating on it for countless hours. It just worked, at least sometimes. Vann pulled fifty thousand over, bringing the indicator up to 170K, and chained down the handle. "Let's go get that coffee," Vann said, wrapping an arm around me and leading me to the dog house cabin that sat behind us. I wearily smiled, knowing we had done all we could do with the tools we had in the hole.

We joined Rikki, who was still sitting inside and had been watching everything. Vann poured our cups as I stared through the doorway at the indicator and wondered if that needle would kick in my favor. I watched without really expecting any positive results, waiting as I listened to the coffee being poured into my cup.

"It don't matter how hard you look at it, it ain't going to move," Vann said as he handed me my cup and observed with me. Maybe I was obsessed. I wanted this fish out of the hole and to go home. I was tired of this well kicking our ass.

"Yeah, I know, but I can dream."

He just laughed at me. "You had better stop dreaming, hand. It ain't coming out, at least not anytime soon."

"Yeah, you may be right. That's why I got that washover shoe in the back of my truck and wash pipe on the way."

"You really plan on milling over that fish in the horizontal?"

"Don't have much of a choice. It's not the most ideal plan, but it's what we're left with."

He chewed down on his lip and glanced back at me. "You know what, Wyatt?"

"What?"

He slammed his hand down on the cold steel of the knowledge box. "Fishing sucks!"

I breathed in the aroma of Folger's as I took another sip. "Yeah, it sure does." I walked over and stared at the indicator, thinking that maybe I could mentally move the needle if I looked hard enough.

Vann came up beside me. "Nothing?"

"Not a thing."

"What you wanna do, boss?"

"I don't know yet." I thought about my options, how they were so few, and decided to change the subject. "You got family, Vann?"

He looked up at me in puzzlement, probably wondering why I would be interested. "Yeah, my wife just gave birth to our baby girl. Got three boys, but this is our first girl." His face started to glow as he finished speaking.

"You excited?" I asked, already knowing the answer.

His head bobbed with excitement as he smiled in response. "I never thought I would get a chance to be a part of something so pure, so special, so surreal. She will be so much better than me and worlds above than those crazy boys." He stared me dead in the eye. "I just want her to have a good life, to live the life I couldn't. I wanna give her that. I just hope I can."

I sipped my coffee as I listened carefully. "I'm sure you can." I contemplated on what the life was he couldn't live and why but held my tongue.

"I sure hope so. I just wish I could get out of the field and be home with my family for a change." He seemed deep in thought as I took another sip of coffee. "Do you ever think that's why we were put here on this earth, just to give our kids more than what we have, more than we could ever have dreamed of?"

"It's got merit, but I don't know if it's the only reason we were put here on this earth."

"Well, it sure seems to be for me. I want them to have it better than I did."

"I've definitely heard of worse plans."

"You got kids, Wyatt?"

"No, can't say I do. Came close one time."

"You will. I can see it in you. You'll make a great father."

"I hope so. Things just don't always play out how you want them to. Oilfield life isn't always what a woman wants."

He nodded his head in agreement. "This is true, my friend; this is true."

I thought on his earlier, bigger question, the one I didn't know if I really wanted to talk about. "I don't have it all figured out, but I think we were put here for something bigger than just having kids."

"What do you think it is, then?" He asked.

I thought on the question and answered it with a

question. "Are you a Christian?"

"That question sure seems to be getting asked of me quite frequently lately." He replied.

"It's a fair question when talking about the meaning of life."

He was quiet as he seemed to struggle to find a response. "My wife has been talking a lot about this Christian faith, and I gotta tell you, I'm not interested."

"I understand that, but if you ever get curious, I got a Bible with your name on it."

He nudged me. "Don't hold on to it for too long."

"I don't plan to."

He smiled at me and gestured at his cup, signaling that he needed a refill. "You need any more?"

"Yeah, I'll take another cup." I handed him my cup and glanced over at the needle of the indicator again. It hadn't budged—still holding strong at 170.

Rikki's loud mouth came to life and yelled across the doghouse to me. "What you wanna do, Wyatt?"

I glared toward him as I stated the obvious. "I wanna unscrew and come out of the hole."

He crossed his arms over the rolling flabs of his chest as his brain tried to form an original thought. "But we moved her a foot?"

"Yeah, but not an inch since."

"I feel like if we came out of the hole now, it would be too soon," he said.

"I just feel like we are wasting time if we continue jarring," I retorted.

His eyes glared up to mine. "You gotta remember this is my well."

"I don't think we were debating that."

"I just wanna make sure."

I tried to hide any mockery in my voice as I spoke. "Okay, now that you are sure, can we continue on deciding what to do?" He continued to glare through me. Apparently, I wasn't very good at hiding mockery.

"I gotta make a phone call."

"All right. We'll keep jarring." I watched as Rikki pulled out a flip phone from his coveralls and went to the other side of the doghouse to talk in peace.

Vann set his cup of coffee down and followed me out to the driller's stand. He grabbed hold of the brake handle and looked at me. "All right. Whatta you wanna do, boss?"

"Let's bring her on down and cock the jars." As the words left my lips, Vann was already lowering pipe. My gaze locked on the indicator losing weight faster than usual.

"Hold it right there, Vann." He pushed the handle down, stopped the drill string, and shot me a confused look.

I pointed to the indicator. "Ever seen that before?" The weight was falling off without the drill pipe lowering. The needle dropped below 120k.

"Only when we are freed up."

"I don't think we are, though."

"What you wanna do, then?" he asked.

I looked back in the doghouse. "Rikki! Get out here!"

"What!"

"I need you to make a decision on *your* well!" He slapped the phone shut and straggled over next to us. We watched as the indicator steadily moved lower without the drill string moving with it. I racked my brain on anything that would make the drill string lighter without us doing anything to it.

"What the hell you want me to do about that? Figure it out, *tool hand*!"

"That's what I figured. I thought it was your fucking well?"

His gaze burned right through me as he exploded in anger. "What the hell are you good for?" He turned away and paced away a few steps before turning back toward me. "You're a sack of shit! You want me to do your job and mine! Just do your fucking job!"

I exploded. "That's what I'm trying to do if you would shut your fucking mouth! Every move I make you want to approve! So approve!" In reply, he staggered around me, shoved Vann out of the way, and grabbed the brake handle.

"You want me to run this shit show? I'll run it! You sons of bitches!" Vann and I watched as he fumbled with the controls and started burying the drill string deeper. "Let's get jarring, boys!" We stepped back to watch the show and get some space as the needle continued falling.

I frantically calculated while I stood there watching a mad man run the rig. "Vann, have that derrick hand check on the pits."

"What for?"

I turned sharply. "Just do it!" The words spurted out more abruptly than I wanted. Vann picked up and phoned the derrick hand and waved me over.

"He said the pits are gaining volume at an alarming rate! And the shakers are starting to overflow!"

"Damn it!" I turned to Rikki, who was still burying pipe and trying to get the jars cocked, and noticed liquid starting to bubble up over the rotary. "Rikki! We gotta shut this bitch in!"

He leaned his head back. "Why we gotta do that?" As soon as the words left his mouth, dark drilling fluid started spewing out of the top of the drill pipe. This was our warning from the angel of death; if we didn't get control in the next 15 seconds there would be a good chance that we weren't going to.

"Rikki, we got to get that TIW screwed in!"

"I will just come down and screw into the pipe," he said. I watched him fumble with the controls, trying to bring the top drive lower without having any slips to stop the drill string. I looked back at Vann. He was screaming over the phone to his motorman to get the bag shut before it started spewing uncontrollably up the backside. I heard the door slam open and looked back at Dakotah standing in the door way. "What you need, boss?" he asked me. I didn't reply; I didn't know what help he could be right this second.

Raindrops of drilling fluid and oil splattered on my hard hat as I yelled out, "Rikki! Let me have the brake!"

"Go fuck yourself! You are not even allowed on the brake!"

"It's on you if we lose this well!"

"It's always on me! It's my fucking well!"

I felt the oil drops picking up momentum as they splattered my hardhat. It was true, my job classification prohibited me from legally touching driller controls, especially in a time of chaos. Even if I had built the rig and invented the controls, I would have still been fired for running the rig, even if I saved the day. Those thoughts rang in the back of my mind as I debated the scenario and went with the best decision I could muster. "Vann! Get on that fucking brake!" He looked my way and slammed the receiver down as the drilling fluid started to blow out from drill pipe like a fountain and coat the derrick pitch black. He rushed to the brake like an all-star running back and easily pushed Rikki out of the way. I watched as Rikki shoved at Vann and tried to regain control of the brake. Vann's years of roughnecking and considerable bulk prevented Rikki from budging him. While he maintained control, he looked over at Rikki as if to say, "Please do it again."

Vann dialed in controls and buried pipe lower as he turned to Dakotah. "I need that TIW valve ready to be stabbed." The brakes screeched as Vann slammed down and chained off the handle, stopping the drum of the draw works and holding the drill string at floor level. I ran out to help Dakotah stab the TIW safety valve. Oil and drilling fluid started painting the sky as it spurted 30 feet above us. The derrick, and every piece of equipment, was becoming covered in oil and invert at a very rapid pace. Dakotah bear-hugged the three-foot, two hundred-pound safety valve off the rack and brought it to the floor as I grabbed part of the valve, trying to find the room to assist the big Indian. Vann ran out to the floor to join us. We each grabbed the handles on the side as we desperately looked at one another, oil dripping off every one of our faces.

"Ready?" I shouted. We picked up the valve with ease from the strength of the three of us and pushed our way toward the spewing drill pipe and waited for an open moment to stab the valve.

I heard Dakotah's voice cry out over the noise of what sounded like jet engines ready to explode. "Ready!" We picked up the valve chest high and moved forward, stabbing the valve and immediately rotating it, passing the handles to the right. I felt relief as a thread grabbed, and we furiously tried to rotate to tighten up the valve to the drill pipe. Thick liquid started to soak my pants and go inside of my boots. It felt as if a surging wave was rising over our boots. The pressure from the backside was starting to gain momentum. I looked over at Vann and tried to yell over the sound of gas blowing out as if jet engines were sucking air. "Did your motorman shut that backside?"

"He said he did!" Vann leaned into the valve, pushing his weight against the handle as he spoke, desperately trying to get another thread as pressure picked up and gas started shooting out the top of the valve. "Wyatt! Go and double-check that backside!"

My nose sensed the ominous stench of rotten eggs, and a shiver flowed through my spine as I looked at Vann. He must have smelled it too; his face was as white as a ghost, as I'm sure mine also was. It was the smell of hydrogen sulfide—a gas that could kill a crew in three seconds flat. The valve only had one thread screwed in, and I didn't want the pressure to spin it back out, but I started feeling as if I didn't have a choice but to check on the backside. I leaned into the valve as I felt another thread take. "You got this?"

"Yeah, we got this. Go check on that backside!" I backed away from the valve and hurriedly made it past the driller's stand when the sound of an explosion filled my ears, and the force of the pressure slammed me against the steel of the doghouse. I felt a sharp pain shoot through my leg and the taste and thickness of my own blood mixed with oil filled my mouth. My body went limp with shock and pain as I collapsed with a darkness covering my eyes.

CHAPTER 19

When I awoke, destruction was abound. Gas and oil continued to blow, and my heart sank as I looked across the floor at the derrick leg that held Vann at the bottom of it. Blood flowed from his skull, and the valve lay on top of him. I pressed my fingers to his neck trying to take a pulse but there was none. I looked over trying to spy Dakotah, but I couldn't see him through the spew of oil and the fog of gas. There was no time to think about anything. I struggled to my feet, staggered downstairs to the accumulator, grabbed hold of the handle that read *Blind Rams* and fiercely pulled. I listened as the hydraulics pushed the rams against the steel of the drill pipe, which produced a burst of pressure and sheared the pipe in half, closing off the well. I heard the beautiful sound of silence as the well went eerily quiet. The rams had successfully sheared the drill pipe and closed the flow, returning the oil and gas back to the hell it came from.

I went back up to the floor and looked around for Dakotah. I found him on the opposite side of the floor from Vann. He was lying on the iron floor, starting to wake up. His big Indian body bore the brunt of the blow, but he hadn't been thrown into anything, nor had the valve slammed across his skull, although he was still bleeding from his forehead and drenched in oil.

I bent down to the big Indian as he was trying to shake off his injuries. "How you doing?" I asked. He took a moment, closed his eyes, and shook his head as if trying to shake the fog away. Then, he grabbed hold of my forearm and started trying to pull himself up. My body almost toppled over from the weight of the big Indian, and it took every ounce of the strength I had to assist the 300-pound Indian to his feet.

"How's Vann?"

I feared the reaction and didn't know what to expect from the big Indian, but after a deep breath, I softly muttered, "He's dead." I watched the Indian crumble. His legs gave out, and he fell back down to the iron floor. He buried his head into his knees and began to softly weep. After about a minute, he looked back up at me with an accusing glare.

"Why didn't you do something?" He began to struggle to his feet. I tried to find an answer but couldn't articulate one. "Answer me, tool man! Why didn't you do something?" He walked toward me and backed me into the steel of the draw works, putting his finger firmly into my chest. "You could have done something!" His fist balled up, and I felt trapped as he got closer and his belly pushed me harder against the draw works. "Answer me, tool man!" I felt the venom of his spit splatter on my cheek, and his eyes turned dark as he demanded answers. There was nothing I could say. I knew I should have never let Rikki touch the brake. I should have pushed him out of the way before Vann ever had to. I should have acted sooner instead of worrying about Rikki making a decision. I knew I could come up with many excuses, but there were none that would free me from a man dying on my watch. I watched the big Indian pick up an eight-pound sledgehammer that had been strewn across the floor from the blowout.

Bam! I moved my head just in time as the hammer pounded into the draw works beside my head, denting the thick-walled steel. He followed up with a side swing that landed right on my hipbone. Pain coursed throughout my body as I took a fall against the cold iron floor. I looked up as the big Indian raised the sledge over my defenseless body. I wanted to slither away and find some sort of defense, but I could barely move from the pain in my hip, and there were no other tools of defense in reach. I felt powerless as I awaited my fate.

Bam! The steel of the sledge contacted the iron within two inches of my face, and I felt a ricochet of steel chips spark into my eye. I squinted at the big Indian, stung by the steel slivers piercing my eye. His body slackened, he dropped the sledge, and the rage that had consumed him seemed to vanish as quickly as it had come. He held a hand out to me. "Come on, tool man." I grabbed hold of his hand, still unsure if he was sincere or wanted to pound me into oblivion. He pulled me to my feet as I fought the pain in my hip and my eye. I limped over with Dakotah to Vann's body leaning against the A-leg of the oil-drenched derrick. Dakotah bent down and pushed the valve off his body and grasped his meaty hands around the back of the driller and clenched him close to his chest and wept. I stared at the murder outline of Vann's body on the wall. The small section on the A-leg was the only thing on the rig floor that wasn't covered in sludge due to his body hitting the iron.

"I'm sorry. It wasn't your fault." The big Indian stared at me, and I grabbed the paw he stuck out to me even though I knew he was wrong.

I limped forward as I replied. "Thank you. Let's go check on Rikki and get the hell out of here."

"Ok, tool man." He patted me on the back as I limped down the stairs with him following. Pain raged through my body, but had no comparison to the ache in my heart for

Vann's wife, sons, and his little girl who would never truly know her daddy.

Rikki had fallen down the beaver slide when the valve blew off and had gotten slightly banged up, but other than that, he looked okay, no open wounds, but he was out cold laying as a dead fish. As the big Indian and I stood over the lard ass, I raised an open hand behind my shoulder and let it come down, forcing my palm across his face hard enough to sting and leave a smudgy oil print of my hand on his face. "Rise and shine, sunshine,"

He raised his head and wearily opened his eyes. "What the hell did you slap me for?" he asked.

I didn't have to respond. Dakotah stood with his arms folded against his chest and spoke for me. "You will be very fortunate if that's all you get."

"Come on let's go. We got some phone calls to make," I said.

. . . .

I watched as the early morning sun rose behind the derrick. Zebb and Bryant pulled into location in Zebb's Dodge and pulled beside mine. I limped out. Neither muttered a greeting. They were too stunned; they merely stood there as they looked at me in my drenched coveralls and dried blood down the side of my cranium and then glanced back at the rig.

Finally, Bryant walked toward me and wrapped his arm around my shoulder; his spotless polo sleeve became stained with oil from the back of my neck. "You all right, brother?"

My eyes started to weep as I tried to find words. "I think so." He guided me to Rikki's trailer as Zebb held open the door, and Bryant sat my dirty body down on Rikki's smooth leather couch.

"Hey, what the hell? He's filthy." Rikki said. He himself was sporting brand new coveralls.

"This is true," Bryant replied as I leaned back into the cushion and rested my head against the wall without the ability to muster words. It idly occurred to me that I was going to leave a big oil stain on the wall too.

The room filled with local superintendents, engineers, safety guys, paramedics, and the chief of police, who sat close to three OSHA inspectors. Bryant and Zebb remained standing. I looked at Rikki and spied my handprint still glowing red across his face and immediately wished I hadn't stopped with the kindness of an open hand slap.

When the meeting formally started, one of the OSHA inspectors was the first to speak. "I believe everyone is aware of what has happened, including there being one death on site. We will be starting an investigation immediately and hope to find no acts of negligence." The room was solemn since there was little to say. He looked directly at Bryant. "We will be needing all of your man's job notes and logs."

"Sure thing." He looked toward me as if to silently ask and plead that I had them typed already. I nodded in response.

The room sat in deafening silence until the company superintendent leaned forward in his chair and spoke to Bryant. "You and your men are officially run off."

"For what?"

"Not for the accident. We haven't got to the bottom of that yet, but from what Rikki has told us, your guy has been insubordinate the whole job and chose to slap Rikki forcefully." I felt a weight being pushed against my chest as the blame continued to pour, and I tried to find words to respond, but as I leaned forward and opened my mouth, Bryant motioned for me to shut up.

"He was trying to make sure the son of a bitch was still alive."

"It was more force than necessary. Regardless, Rikki has said he has had nothing but problems with your men."

Zebb pointed toward Rikki and spoke fiercely. "Your man is a fucking idiot! We did nothing wrong, and I guarantee you that Wyatt did everything in his power to keep this from happening."

"It doesn't matter, it's been decided."

"This is BULLSHIT!" Zebb replied.

Bryant looked at him and spoke like an old sage. "It doesn't matter what this guy says, Zebb. He has no clue what happened out here; he is taking a dumbass's word without investigation. What does that make him?" Zebb seemed to calm as Bryant turned back toward Rikki and the superintendent and respectfully replied, "Gentleman, I believe this meeting is over."

The main OSHA inspector stood and shook hands with all of us and nodded at Bryant. "We will be in touch."

CHAPTER 20

"All in!" We sat in Bryant's basement around a card table as I pushed my chips to the middle of the table and took a slug of Jack Daniels. Toby had just flopped the 2, 3, and 4 of diamonds, and I held the 5 and 6 of clubs. Easy straight.

Bryant sat his glass down on the card table and pushed his chips over mine. "Call."

"Come on, you guys ain't got shit, and you know it. Chasing straights, the both of you," Toby blurted out as he folded his cards and took a sip of water.

I laughed in response. "You're just mad 'cause you don't drink."

He chuckled back to me. "Maybe." He glanced across the table toward Zebb. "Whatcha going to do, big man?"

Zebb folded. "Too rich for my blood."

Bryant smiled at me and gestured for me to turn over my cards. I poured whiskey into my glass and then splashed some coke on top of the poison. "You first," I retorted as I gestured back at him. He flopped a pair of eights over as Toby stood up from his chair. "You went in with that shit?" I chuckled and flopped over the five and six of diamonds. Bryant just shrugged.

"We still got two more cards."

Toby just shook his head in disbelief as he burned a card and flipped the next one. An eight appeared from the deck. I took another swig, and the ash taste of Jack lingered. Bryant motioned, "Next." Toby burned another and we all stared in disbelief as the other eight appeared. Bam! Bryant slapped the pathetic card table, and my drink toppled over and began soaking into his basement carpet. "I told you!" He raked in the chips as I sat back in disbelief and took another slug.

"I can't believe that shit!" Toby said as he adjusted his ball cap.

"Just my luck, my friend." I leaned back in my chair and looked toward Bryant. "Have you heard back from that OSHA inspector?"

"Yeah, they're done. You are cleared and Rikki is fired. Apparently, your friend Dakotah spoke up and changed the outcome in your favor."

I wasn't too surprised, but the news did ease my nerves about the situation. "Right on." I grabbed my glass off the floor and picked off some dog hair from Bryant's Great Dane that was stuck to it. I was approaching my limit, and honestly, I probably shouldn't have had another. Still, I was feeling celebratory, so I poured myself one.

Bryant grabbed the neck of the bottle of Jack and poured his own glass half full.

"Whatever happened to that well?" I asked.

"Apparently, they are still fighting pressure on and off but finally got a snubbing unit on the well." I glanced at Zebb. He shook his head in disbelief at their stupidity of such a delay in action; it was what we had wanted to do in the beginning. "They have run off two more fishing companies due to inexperience." He sat back in pleasure as he pursed his lips to his glass. "That superintendent keeps leaving messages on my phone, trying to get us back out there."

I busted a laugh. Zebb shook his head and chuckled with me. "What do you say, youngster, you want to go back out there?"

My laugh went deeper at the silliness of the question. "Hell, no!" We laughed at the irony of it all.

I felt the pain in my hip as I adjusted my seating. "I have been thinking about that well, though, as you can imagine." It was true that it had consumed my thoughts, and every time I moved, my hip reminded me of it. "I think the whole problem was communication." I chased my thoughts with whiskey as Zebb spoke up.

"No shit, Sherlock."

Bryant chuckled. "You think?"

Toby stared toward me.

I sat my glass down. "No, you don't follow, not communication, but COM-MU-NI-CA-TION. You have that frack job just a mile down the road. If that pressure kept coming online then offline, it would make sense because it was every time they fracked a stage."

Bryant's eyes widened as he followed along. A dawning awareness caused Zebb's head to pipe up. Toby leaned back in thought. Zebb leaned forward and looked at me. "I think you are fucking right." He slapped his hand on the table and then rubbed both hands through his hair. "I can't believe we didn't think of this before, we were so busy trying to fix the well that we didn't think about another one actually causing the problem." I sat back and awaited Bryant's response.

"Let's go out there."

"Now?" I asked

"Yes, now!" he replied. I looked over at Toby, the only sober one. "What do you think?"

"Well, I think you are probably dead on with the communication theory. It only makes sense."

Zebb stroked his fingers over his forehead and through his hair. "Holy shit, I think you're right."

Bryant, Zebb, and I stood up. I felt the pangs in my hip reminding me of the hell that well had borne. "All right, let's go." Bryant said. Toby spoke up.

"I don't think that's a good idea. You guys are plastered."

"So what? We just solved the fucking problem! We could walk in there bare-ass naked, barely able to walk, and they would love us."

"Come on, let 'em wait it out one more night." Toby said. We all grumbled in slight frustration at the wisdom of the sober one, but as my hand wrapped around my glass we nodded and acquiesced to his better judgment.

"I'm going upstairs to get some ice," I said. I dismissed myself and grabbed my crutches as they continued their game.

. . . .

Her head of red hair turned toward me and away from the TV while I crutched up the last stair. "Hey, there. How's it going down there?" Cady asked, she was still awake awaiting Jessica's arrival to Williston.

"Pretty good. I think we just solved the issue on that well."

"That's good. What was it?"

"There was a frack job about a mile down the road, and every time they kicked their pumps on, the pressure would communicate and come into our well. Their pressure reached upwards of nine thousand pounds, and we got our share of it. When it communicated, it collapsed our casing on top of my tools." I sat down on the couch and stretched my leg out. "We should have thought of it sooner, but it hasn't been an issue in North Dakota in years 'cause the wells used to be so far apart, but now they are getting put right on top of one another." She nodded in agreement. I was never quite sure if she totally understood what we talked about, but she was always supportive. I leaned back and took a sip of whiskey as I heard a knock at the door; Cady went to get it. She opened it up, and I watched as she and Jessica got acquainted. Jessica sat her bags down and looked me over with my crutches leaning against the couch.

"What happened to you?" she asked as she pulled up a chair for me to rest my leg on and took a seat next to me. I hadn't mentioned anything about what had happened and knew I would have a lot to explain. I had my own communication problem, it seemed.

EPILOGUE

That next morning, Bryant, Zebb, and I went out to the rig and talked with the new consultant on location, who was quite pleasant. He, along with the superintendent, took little convincing to shut the frack job down. Once the frack was shut down, the pressure stopped immediately, and a breath of fresh air reached all of us. The superintendent thanked us profusely and offered to continue to let us work on the well. We accepted—with a few conditions that he agreed to, along with some price changes in favor of Anderson Oil Tools.

The job continued for another week once we took over and went fairly smoothly. We were able to wash over the packer after cutting out additional drill pipe and milled up the casing that had collapsed around the packer from the pressure surges. We got all the tools out of the hole and patched up the collapsed section. It was a very positive thing for Anderson Oil Tools and our phone started ringing off the hook once word began to spread, which did not hurt Bryant's feelings since he received a well-deserved raise for his handling of OSHA and the entire situation.

I got a thank you letter from the CEO of Anderson Oil Tools, who thanked me for successfully and professionally dealing with the well from hell. He also sent me a package with the second smoothest leather tally book I had ever felt. It portrayed a picture of a tool hand on a rig floor setting a tool downhole with a pipe wrench and had the words "Gotta Feel It" above it.

I tried talking to Zebb again about his dreams of Jesus, but he didn't want to hear anything about the man I called God. His dreams have continued, but he says he is able to sleep through them most of the time. He also said that he has cracked the Bible a time or two but really didn't find it helpful as of yet. He tried to give it back to me, but I wouldn't accept it. We went to Vann's funeral. It was a closed casket, distressing and tragic. I laid the Bible I had saved for him on top of his casket as they laid him to rest and gave a separate one to his little girl. My heart still burned for him.

Bryant gave us both a week off after the job was completed. I went back Dillon to hang out in the mountains of Montana and to rest with Jessica and have that second date. She helped nurse me back to health and dragged me to the doctor several times over. My hip ended up being fractured, and my eye still held a sliver of steel and was starting to make the left side of my head go numb. I had a lot to explain, and she made me promise I would start telling her when these sorts of things happen. I tried to explain the unusual circumstances, but she wouldn't buy any of my excuses. I rented a small cabin nestled in the mountains and spent much of my time on the porch drinking Jack Daniels and reading my Bible, about which the doctors said only one of the two was helpful for my recovery. They were probably right, but it didn't change my activities. I couldn't walk without crutches yet, so I usually hopped around the property and collected rocks and agates. Vann's death still bothered me and consumed my thoughts. I tried to convince myself that it wasn't my fault, but I couldn't quite get there, and I wondered if I ever would. As I pondered and played back the events of the well, it was easier with a glass of Jack, and it usually called for a refill if I thought too much on it.

I called up Bryant and requested an additional week off due to my slow recovery. Bryant granted it with no questions asked and said that Zebb called in and requested the same, although he didn't have much cause for another week off. Bryant granted it anyhow. He said that he couldn't get any information out of Zebb about where he was hiding. We both speculated but truly had no idea.

Toby traveled over for a visit and brought me a case of Jack and smoked brisket from The Branding Iron. He had gotten word that Jessica didn't encourage drinking Jack Daniels and reading scripture and thought my supply might be getting low. It was tough to get the gumption to make it into town, and I was glad to see him. We mostly sat on the porch together and talked about old wells we had worked together. He brought a rifle, and we set up a makeshift range on the side of a mountain and took turns shooting empty Jack Daniel's bottles.

Jessica stopped by after Toby had been gone a couple days and said she brought a friend. She helped me hobble to the car. I was really drunk and confused because there was nobody was in the backseat. She opened the door.

I looked down at the red and white McNab border collie sporting a newly bought pink collar lying in the backseat. "A puppy?" I asked. Her nose to her forehead was white; burnt red circled her eyes. Her oversized ears sat propped up as if she was a miniature Great Dane. I watched as she reached her hind leg up and scratched them. "She's got fleas." She stopped scratching and sat straight and stared at me. I turned to Jessica. "I don't have time for a dog."

"I'll watch her when you are gone." The puppy stared

out the back window and then back to me. I looked her over as she sat upright staring into me. I reached down and scratched behind her oversized ears and sighed.

"What's her name?" I asked.

"That's up to you."

I breathed heavily, crossed my arms, and took another sip of Jack. "Annie." The pup stared into me, wagging her tail. I took one more sip and pondered the name as I felt a warm hand slip into mine and a kiss brush my cheek. It was official.